I couldn't fall asleep. From my window I could see the shadows shift in the garden. The bushes rustled. Twigs snapped, and as a thin cloud passed across the moon, I could see the glint of eyes watching. All around the house, the foxes had gathered. They knew, just like all animals knew, that we weren't another ordinary family moving in. That we weren't like the other neighbours, tucked up tight in their beds, dreaming of jobs and school and breakfast, and all the other ordinary things normal people dream of. No, we were the Bradley family and we were different.

*Also by Amber Lee Dodd*

We Are Giants
Lightning Chase Me Home

Amber Lee Dodd

the THIRTEENTH
HOME of NOAH
BRADLEY

■ SCHOLASTIC

Published in the UK by Scholastic Children's Books, 20XX
Euston House, 24 Eversholt Street, London, NW1 1DB, UK
A division of Scholastic Limited.

London – New York – Toronto – Sydney – Auckland
Mexico City – New Delhi – Hong Kong

ISBN 978 1407 18944 4

A CIP catalogue record for this book
is available from the British Library.

Printed by CPI Group (UK) Ltd, Croydon, CR0 4YY
Papers used by Scholastic Children's Books are made
from wood grown in sustainable forests.

1 3 5 7 9 10 8 6 4 2

www.scholastic.co.uk

For Mum, Dad,
Ryan and Asha

# PROLOGUE

Once there was a family who followed the North Star across the ocean. Its bright light led them away from war-torn lands and promised new fields and forests to call their own. But the family sailed too far. To an island in the cold north, far from the light of the sun.

There, only the moon shone, and the wind always blew, and the ocean always churned, and the snow and ice always fell. Only the people of the hills knew how to live there, and they were a dangerous people, of old magic and grudges that never went unpunished. So the family built their house far from the hills, in the valley under the stars. But the stars were jealous and swept down from the sky and tore the house apart. So they built another by the sea, but the ocean decided to claim it for its own and washed it away. So they built another in the slopes of a hill. But this was grey wolf territory and every night they came scratching at the door. So they built another high up the mountain, but the frost watched the happy family and wanted to join them, so it crept in under their windows, crawled under the doors, seeped in through the roof, until the house turned to ice.

At last, the oldest son travelled six days and six nights to ask the people in the hills for their help. He arrived cold and hungry and hardly able to stand. And the people from the hills took pity on the young, frail boy, and so weaved their magic into four gifts, one for each of the family. For the mother they made a fire poker that could conjure a fire that would never go out, keeping the snow and frost at bay. For the father they crafted a lantern that once lit could control the tides, protecting them from the temperamental sea. For the girl they built a weathervane that could channel the wind and lightning to protect against the mischievous stars. And finally, for the boy, they made a door knocker that could summon the animals of the earth for protection from the wolves.

The people of the hills gave these gifts willingly. But they issued a warning, too.

"Use these gifts wisely," they said. "For like you,

these gifts are stronger together. Remember, we can ask for their return at any time."

The family were grateful. Barely daring to hope, they built a new house, in the valley this time. And with all four gifts united under one roof their powers began to grow. Soon the family could wield near complete control over the elements.

But magic is dangerous; it whispers to those who would be good and strong and makes them weak and unwise. The mother came to believe the small wooden house wasn't good enough for them. She wanted more. So the family went to the forest for trees to build more floors and bigger bedrooms.

But that wasn't enough. The boy wanted stables for his horses. So they went back to the forest to build them.

And then the daughter wanted a grand hall to dance in. So they emptied the quarries of stone to build a floor fit for a thousand kings to dance across.

And soon after the father wanted an atrium that looked up into the bright skies and darkest nights that unfolded on the edge of the world. So they emptied the beaches of sand to make a giant glass ceiling.

And after all that, the valley was stripped bare until not a hare, rabbit or fox was left.

The people from the hills had watched as their

gifts were misused. Finally, they realized enough was enough. So they called to the wolves from the hills and howled to the depths of the ocean and cried to the stars and the ice to take back the house their gifts had helped build.

But the magic in the house was strong and the family knew how to wield it. The wolves could not get past the door. The waves could not reach the house and the falling stars and ice could not break through the roof.

At last, they called the black birds of the north to gather the North Wind. And the North Wind, once gentle and welcoming, turned against the family. It pulled apart the house. As they fled, each member of the family took their gift, before going their separate ways to follow the North Star again.

But the people from the hill do not forgive or forget so easily. They cursed the family to be rootless as they once were, chased by the birds of the north, who would bring misfortune to any place they came to call home for so long as they held on to magic. Until, united again with their true strength, they could bring the curse to a close.

# CHAPTER 1

It was past midnight when we first arrived at Verity Close. The moon hung big and bright in the sky and the street was lined with a parade of foxes, their golden eyes glinting in the darkness. Like they had been waiting for us. The close was quiet otherwise. With curtains drawn across every window – every window but one. One bedroom light lit the shadowy street. Someone was watching us, then. Wondering who could possibly be moving in this late. I could tell strangers were unusual here. Because Verity Close was a nice normal neighbourhood. Like one you would draw in a picture. Identical, neat three-bedroom houses all lined in a row, each with a pink magnolia tree in the front garden. There was only one house out of place, the one at the end of the street. The one that would be ours.

Even from our van I could see a garden filled with junk, tiles missing from the roof and a cracked window covered with newspaper. But I didn't care about that. I didn't even care that we had driven all day without stopping. That Dad's face was lined with worry and Mum's knuckles were white and still gripped to the steering wheel. I only cared about one thing.

"Are we safe now?" I asked Mum.

She didn't reply right away. Her eyes darted nervously to the rear-view mirror before she asked,

"Can you see anything, Noah?"

I wiped a clean spot on the fogged-up back window. We had lost the black birds from the north over the Tyne Bridge. That didn't mean we were safe though. We could only outrun our bad luck for so long. But under the amber street lights the world was still.

"I need a wee," my brother, Billy, whispered.

Mum turned to us and the van let out a little groan. It was a small miracle we had been able to fit everything in this time. Despite being expert packers and not owning anything but what Mum called "the essentials", we still had four large suitcases, Dad's toolbox and one bag each filled with our emergency kit. Or in Billy's case, three mega tubes of Smarties and a ferret named Arnold. And strapped to the roof was Mum's special wooden trunk. It was very old and had been in our family for generations. In every home we'd lived in, it had been hidden away and kept locked. Mum wore the little silver key to it around her neck. She was fiddling with it now.

"OK. Are you ready to see your new home?" Mum asked, putting on her overly bright happy voice that made her sound like a children's TV presenter.

Billy and I nodded. Dad said nothing. All the way here Mum had talked about how great this place would be. That things would be different here. But I'd heard it all before. I was only twelve but I'd already lived in twelve different homes. And even Dad, who usually joined in to cheer us up, seemed to think this was one too many moves, and had spent the journey in silence.

I looked at the boarded-up door and newspaper-covered window again. I thought about our last place, a trailer on the edge of a lake. We'd had a big 50-inch TV and a deck for barbecues. This new place looked dark and dingy and there was no deck. But I could see how nervous Billy was, so I tried to copy Mum's TV presenter smile.

"Let's go," I said.

The house was worse up close. The garden was

filled with cat poo and on the door in dirty numbers was the number thirteen. Thirteen! The unluckiest number of them all. It was a very bad sign.

"It's just a bit dirty," Mum said, catching my eye.

She rubbed at the number with the cuff of her jacket. The thirteen turned into an eighteen. I let out a long sigh of relief. I hadn't even realized I'd been holding my breath. Billy reached out and squeezed my hand. He always knew when I was most afraid. If Billy were an animal, he would be an octopus. The octopus has amazing senses even though they're completely deaf. Instead they're able to feel and taste danger before it ever arrives. Just like Billy, who has a sixth sense for when I'm upset, no matter how hard I try to hide it. I squeezed his slightly sticky hand back and Billy signed, "Got you, brother."

Billy's partially deaf, and even though he can hear pretty well with his hearing aids, he likes to sign when he's around a lot of people, or when he's nervous. And arriving in the dead of night to a strange tumbledown house was making us both nervous. Mum rattled the key in the lock and the front door swung open with a groan.

Inside was worse than I had imagined. When Mum flicked on the light, I could see floorboards sticking out at old angles, a grey stain on the ceiling and yellowed peeling wallpaper. And the whole house smelt of old cigarettes and pee. I wrinkled my nose.

"It needs a little work doing," Mum said, still cheerful. "The last person to live here let it go a bit before he. . ." She stopped short.

I knew what she was going to say: before he died. This was a dead person's house. I hugged my duffel bag and thought again of our shiny, clean trailer by the water.

"We just need to use a bit of imagination. Bit of new paint. Some furniture. Your dad can fix anything, isn't that right?" Mum said, turning to Dad.

But Dad only grunted before he walked back to the car to unpack our things. I saw Mum's smile slip for a moment.

"Let's check out the rest," I said to cheer her up.

Mum's face lit up again and she grabbed my and Billy's hands.

"You've got to see the best bit," she said as she pulled us into the hallway. "Stairs."

Billy's eyes lit up.

"We have *stairs*," he said excitedly before flying up them.

We followed Billy up to the big bedroom at the front of the house. He was spinning across the floor, his arms wide.

"We could fit three bunk beds in here, or two proper beds and a sofa. Or a whole wall of beanbags!" he said breathlessly.

"Actually, I was thinking just one bed. Noah's," Mum said from behind me.

"I get my own room?" I said.

Me and Billy had always shared a room. Which had been fun at first, but not so great when you're twelve years old and your younger brother's eight and must pee at least ten times a night.

"But what about me?" Billy whined.

"Well, I was thinking, since you're so small, we could put you in the cupboard," Mum said.

"I don't wanna go in a cupboard! Noah, don't let her put me in a cupboard," Billy said.

He's not very good at telling when people are teasing.

"Just show him his room already," Dad said, hauling Mum's heavy trunk up the stairs.

Billy bounced off with Mum to the room at the end of the corridor, where I could hear his gasps of "whoa" and "awesome" and "I can see the kitchen from the hole in the floor." I stayed in the big room, taking in the moonlight coming through the window. My very own room. Maybe, I thought, just maybe, 18 Verity Close wasn't so bad after all. I knew that was a dangerous thought to have. I couldn't let myself get used to this place. In the end, no matter where we went, we could never stay longer than a year. And even that was pushing it. Sometimes the curse chased us down sooner. But no matter when it happened, it was always the same way. First came the bad omens. Like black cats crossing your path, mirrors breaking or strange weather like snow in summer. But they're subtle and easily missed or ignored. So sometimes it wasn't until we saw the black birds from the north that we knew we were in danger. Because after the birds came the accidents.

"How long do you think we'll stay this time?" I asked Dad as he pumped up my inflatable mattress.

But Dad didn't answer.

That night Billy crawled into my bed.

"Don't you like your new room?" I said.

"Yes, it's great. Mum says I can paint it whatever colour I like, so I'm going to paint it yellow. It'll be like living in the middle of the sun," Billy said. He tugged the sleeping bag off me and over himself. "I just thought you might be lonely."

"Billy, you know we can't get to like this place too much, right?" I said, yanking the sleeping bag back. "Because we'll have to move again soon."

"Maybe we won't. Maybe this time it'll be different," Billy said, his hot breath tickling the back of my neck.

"It won't be," I said.

"Why not?"

"You know why not," I said.

Every time we moved Billy would have to be told again. Every first night in a new place he would ask for the story. But tonight, for some reason, I didn't want to tell it.

"Go to sleep," I said.

"I can't, not until you tell the story," Billy said, putting his little arms around my neck.

"If I do, then will you go to sleep?"

Billy nodded.

"OK," I sighed, turning over and pulling the sleeping bag tight around us. "Once there was a family who followed the North Star across the ocean..."

And I began to tell the story that Mum had told us a thousand times and her mother had told her a thousand more. The one that every Bradley knew by heart.

As I spoke, Billy's breathing became soft and even. "But the people from the hill do not forgive or forget so easily. They cursed the family to be rootless as they once were, chased by the birds of the north, who would bring misfortune to any place they came to call home for so long as they held on to magic. Until, united again with their true strength, they could bring the curse to a close," I finished, to the sound of Billy's snores.

I couldn't fall asleep. From my window I could see the shadows shift in the garden. The bushes rustled. Twigs snapped, and as a thin cloud passed across the moon, I could see the glint of eyes watching. All around the house, the foxes had gathered. They knew, just like all animals knew, that we weren't another ordinary family moving in. That we weren't like the other neighbours, tucked up tight in their beds, dreaming of jobs and school and breakfast, and all the other ordinary things normal people dream of. No, we were the Bradley family and we were different.

# CHAPTER 2

There are rules to being a Bradley.

The first one is: you don't talk about the curse to anyone else.

The second is: you don't forget about the curse.

And the third one is: you never, never get attached to where you live.

There is a fourth and final rule, but I'll tell you about it later.

But as the weeks and then months went by in Verity Close, that third rule became harder and harder to stick to.

Because life in Verity Close was *nice*. It was as close to normal as I'd ever had. Our neighbourhood was quiet, the kind of place where nothing strange or extraordinary ever happened. Our neighbours were ordinary. Nobody ever got drunk, or scary, or played their music too loud, like at some of the other places we had stayed. They all did the same thing every day. Like the Kapoors across the street, who always took their daughter, Neena, to school, and old Mrs Havick, who would come around on the weekend for a cup of tea and to talk about all the people she knew who had died. Or Mr Trevor, who every Friday night would come back late and sing show tunes. Me and Mum loved it all so much we started coming up with our own routines. Every Saturday morning, I would load up on sweets from the corner shop, and every Thursday and Sunday, Mum would go to Zumba and coffee with Mrs Kapoor. Dad and Billy hadn't settled in quite as well. I could tell Dad still missed our last place and Billy always took a while to fit in at school. But I knew he would eventually because St Jude's High School was amazing. I already had a group of close mates and a teacher I really liked, and I was sure I was going to win the history prize cup. Which would be a first for any Bradley. We never stayed anywhere long enough to win anything. And I wasn't the only one doing well. Mum was about to be made a manager at the local restaurant where she had been working. It was one of her best jobs ever, because we always ended up with all the leftovers. Which meant we ate fancy desserts nearly every night. But the very best thing was the house itself.

It was no longer a dirty, broken mess. Dad had worked his usual magic. He had fixed the windows and cleared away the rubbish. And after he had fought the overgrown forest out back, we discovered that we had a garden, a real garden! Soon it had a barbecue and a little table and chairs and Mum's herbs and a shed to keep my racing bike in.

Inside, everything was beautiful too. Mum had kept her promise and done our rooms up. We had painted my bedroom forest green and decorated it with jungle leaf curtains. Dad had put up a shelf for all my zoological books and Lego models. He had even framed up pictures from one of my old natural history books. So I had charts of poisonous jellyfish, the beetles of Britain and deadly snakes of Australia on my walls. It was the nicest room I'd ever had.

The rest of the house took more time. But as Mum worked on it, it became almost unrecognizable. Under the horrible yellowed wallpaper, we'd found old wall mouldings that looked like lions. Behind the dirty electric fireplace was a beautiful black iron one with swirly decorations and green and red tiles that shone like jewels. Mum said the house had "strong, old bones". She said a house like that could protect us.

Ever since we had set foot in 18 Verity Close, Mum kept coming up with reasons why this time we wouldn't have to move. This time it would be different. We would finally have a place to make our home. She was so convincing that I almost believed her.

Not quite enough to unpack the duffel bag I hid under my bed. The bag that was always packed in case we had to leave suddenly. The one that held all my most special things in it, like. . .

- An A-Z map of all the places we had lived. Mum bought me one every time we moved. The night after we arrived Mum would sit on my bed and would point out where all the interesting places were in our new city, town or village, like parks or museums, or the local swimming pool. Then she'd plan all these amazing things we could do. When we lived near the beach in Wales, Mum said we'd go shark spotting. And when we lived in France, she said we'd go spit from the top of the Eiffel Tower. My absolute favourite thing to do was visit the local zoo. I had been to eight now. I liked learning about the animals. They came from all around the world, many of them from places that had been devastated. But in a zoo, they were safe. They all had their own habitats. A place where they belonged. Somehow knowing that made me feel better.

- The patchwork blanket that my nana had worked on, and her nana had worked on before her. It had the four magical objects from the Bradley family story embroidered on the corners. When I was small and things got scary, I had crawled under it and imagined that those patches would protect me.

- A penknife Dad gave me for my tenth birthday. It has seven blades that all did different and amazing things. It even had a toothpick!

- My Lego kit of the London skyline. It was my biggest and most impressive Lego kit; it came with a whole book of instructions. Whenever I felt really worried, I'd start on a Lego kit. It always made me feel better. I liked knowing whatever happened, if I just followed the instructions, I'd end up with what was on the front of the box.

- Snacks. When I get worried it feels like I have a growly black bear in my stomach that's constantly hungry. So I need to feed it. And I'd been having to feed it a lot more since Mum and Dad started having their fights.

They never used to fight like this, but now they argued all the time. They would save them up and have them at night when they thought we were asleep, or in the shed where they thought we couldn't hear.

I wondered if all the arguing had to do with the strange letters that kept arriving for Mum, the ones that made her scurry to her room to read in private. Or the time Dad spent on his laptop. He'd snapped it shut when he'd seen me looking but I went back later and logged into his emails. He had loads of emails from one of his old bosses asking him to come work on a building project in Singapore and he said he was "discussing it with his family". So maybe the discussions were the arguments.

Dad's a construction worker, but not a normal one; he works at great heights building skyscrapers. He's built a bit of the Shard in London and repaired the roof of the Sydney Opera House and even helped fix the clock on Big Ben. That's how he and Mum met. Mum had been working in London and she saw him working up there from her office across the road. Mum always said she fell in love with him "because he didn't seem afraid of anything". But Dad didn't seem that brave any more. Or very happy. He walked around with his shoulders slumped and fell asleep on the couch with a beer.

Things between Mum and Dad seemed to get worse the longer we lived at Verity Close. Until one night they had their biggest row ever and they didn't bother keeping their voices down or going to the shed. Billy and I sat at the top of the stairs listening.

"I have to take this job," Dad yelled.

"Like hell you do," Mum roared back.

"If I don't, how are we going afford the next move, and the one after that, and the one after that? Because the way it's going, the next time we might have to live in the van permanently."

"We won't have to move again. Not if I can help it," Mum said.

"You said that last time. The time I spent four months building on the land my grandfather left to me. And for what, Jo? It's flooded. It's gone. All of it." Dad's voice cracked.

"But that was before," Mum said. "Before I found

her. I can stop this thing, I know I can. I just need a little more time—"

But before Mum could finish Dad interrupted.

"No. I can't get my hopes up. It just makes it harder."

When Mum spoke next, her voice was very cold.

"It's not like you didn't know what you were getting into. You married me; you took my family name. I told you exactly what would happen."

"I know," said Dad, and he sounded tired. "And when it was just me and you it was OK, exciting even. But bringing kids into this..."

"Michael, what are you saying?"

"It wasn't so bad when the kids were small. When we could pretend everything was an adventure. But Billy's growing so fast and Noah ... he wants friends, mates, other kids to grow up with. And when I think of their future, running from place to place, never stopping, it breaks me in two."

"You regret our family?" Mum said, her voice low and wounded.

"I just think we should have thought it through," Dad said quietly.

"Well, you're about twelve years too late on that!" Mum yelled.

Then there was a lot of banging and thumping

about and then Mum appeared in her nightgown. Billy and me bolted back into my room and peered through a crack in the door. Mum came storming up the stairs and into her and Dad's room, where she started opening drawers. There was a *thump* as Dad's suitcase bounced down the stairs. And then the hall light went out.

Billy sat on the floor, hugging his knees.

"Hey," I whispered, and then I signed, "Got you, brother."

Billy smiled sadly; he knew what I meant.

"Love you too, brother," he signed back.

Sometimes it's easier to sign something than say it.

The next morning, whilst I was still in bed, Dad came to talk to me. I could tell it was going to be bad news because he stared at me for a long time without saying anything. I wondered what he was thinking when he was looking at me. In loads of ways me and Dad look just the same. We are both blond, very pale and tall. Dad says that's because of our ancient Norse blood. But I'm less Viking warrior and more terrified villager. I have a lot more squidge in the middle than Dad and have inherited Mum's strange green eyes, as well as her very round face. My face is so round that Daniel Starks at one of my old schools used to call me "Moon

Head". I knew Dad didn't see "Moon Head" when he looked at me, but I wasn't sure he saw anything better. These days I was pretty sure all he saw was Noah Bradley, the boy with the curse.

"Noah," Dad said, and then sighed. "Me and your mum. . ."

Dad trailed off before starting again.

"We think it's best if I go take a job away for a bit. My old boss offered me a job I couldn't turn down. It's loads more money than I make here fitting kitchens and conservatories. But it means I'll be working away for a couple of months, in Singapore," Dad said, and then went quiet.

It was the kind of quiet that fills up a room, making it shrink and shrink until you're sure you're going to be swallowed up by it.

"So," Dad said finally. "What do you think?"

"They have flying lemurs in Singapore. Only they're not really lemurs and they don't fly, they glide." It was the only thing I could think of to say.

"Good to know," Dad said, and a smile flickered across his face, before vanishing again into a thin line of worry.

"Noah, whilst I'm gone, I need you to remember the Bradley family rules."

"Yes, Dad," I said.

"Especially the fourth and final rule," Dad said.

"Yes, Dad," I sighed, pulling the bed covers up over my chin.

"I need to know you're taking this seriously, so repeat after me," Dad said, clearing his throat. "The fourth rule is. . ."

"A Bradley must always look out for bad omens. They are the warning signs of the curse's arrival," I mumbled.

"And what should you be looking out for?" Dad asked.

I repeated the list off by heart:

Black cats.

Strange weather.

The sudden appearance of the number thirteen.

Broken mirrors.

"And most importantly?" Dad said.

"The black birds from the north," I finished.

"Good. Now I need you to promise that if you see any of the signs, you'll tell your mum, you'll pack your bags and you'll call me. I'll come straight back," Dad said. "And then we'll leave, before the accidents start to happen."

The thought made my stomach churn. I didn't *want* to leave 18 Verity Close. Not when, for the first time in ages, I felt like a normal twelve-year-old.

Mum was right. This house was different. This house could finally be our home.

"Promise me?" Dad said again. "Please, Noah, this is important. Mum thinks that things will be . . . different this time. But I'm not so sure. Do you promise me you'll keep the fourth rule?"

I nodded my head.

But it turned out I wasn't good at keeping promises, because the day the black birds from the north arrived, I didn't do any of the things Dad had asked.

# CHAPTER 3

It started with a cat. Three weeks after Dad had left for Singapore, I saw it outside the kitchen window. It was big and black, and it sat watching me from the windowsill with its large unblinking yellow eyes. I felt a cool shudder of fear creep down my spine. And I knew Billy felt it too. He had frozen mid-spoonful of cornflakes. I snapped the blinds down.

"Mum!" I yelled.

Mum dashed into the kitchen, her top still half-unbuttoned and her fox-red hair still dripping wet.

"What is it, Noah?" she said, glancing from me to Billy to see if we were hurt.

"Outside. There's a cat," I said.

Mum let out a little laugh of relief.

"Is that all? I thought one of you was on fire."

"Not like an ordinary one, a black one. It's a sign," I said.

I rolled up the blinds to show Mum. The cat was gone. Mum peered out of the window. The garden was still; the sunshine filtered softly through the washing line. The birds sang. Mrs Havick was standing on her patio smoking in her furry slippers, and the faint sound of Mr Trevor doing his vocal warm-up drifted in. The morning wasn't different to any other one at 18 Verity Close.

"Oh, Noah. Your history project is due in today, isn't it? You must be nervous, feeling a bit on edge," Mum said as she began busying herself around the kitchen, noisily filling up the kettle and getting out cups and plates.

"I saw it! Billy did too," I said, turning to him. "Tell her, Billy."

But Billy didn't say anything. He was too busy hiding behind a fort he had built out of cereal boxes and grinding his cornflakes into dust. Billy always hid when he was nervous. Mum smoothed down the back of Billy's impossibly sticky-up red hair and carried on.

"I'm not saying you didn't. But sometimes cats are just cats. Not everything is about our little problem," Mum said.

I stared at Mum. Our problem wasn't *little*. It was huge. It swallowed up houses, flooded boats, swept caravans off hills. It chased us across countries, through cities and towns. And now it was pulling us all apart.

"Dad told me—" I started again, but I saw Mum stiffen.

She hadn't mentioned Dad once since he'd left for Singapore. Her mobile phone had rung a few times but she hadn't answered it. Even when me and Billy Skyped Dad from Mum's computer she hadn't wanted to talk to him.

"I know what your dad told you. But it's my job to worry about these things, not yours," Mum said, and she pulled me over for a cuddle. "And I have everything under control."

I'm too old to be cuddled, so I let her hug me whilst my arms dangled limply by my sides. But even so, I could feel the knot in my stomach loosen.

"You should be worrying about what twelve-year-olds worry about," she went on. "School, friends ... people who are more than friends?"

"Mum!" I said, squirming away.

"Too early, noted." Mum smiled.

Mum has this big wide smile that makes me feel like everything is going to be all right. It's like she has a light in the centre of her that beams out of her face. If she were an animal, she'd be a firefly, which is technically a beetle, but a very special one. Their whole bodies light up. And each firefly has its own completely different flash: some twinkle, some pulse, some create swirls of light, but each one is unique. Just like Mum.

"Which is a real shame," Mum carried on, her smile turning into a naughty grin that made her witchy green eyes twinkle, "because I think Mrs Havick has taken a shine to you. Since she won't stop talking about you."

I smiled. It was true Mrs Havick wouldn't stop talking about me, but not in a good way. I'd once stopped her from coming in with an open umbrella (very bad luck) and she'd got soaked on the doorstep whilst trying to fiddle it shut. Ever since then she'd been inventing ridiculous things about me to complain about.

"I hear him at night. He walks with the big feet. He snores like a Russian bear in winter, he makes the house shake. One of these days it will fall down," Mum said, doing a wicked impression of Mrs Havick.

I burst out laughing. Billy snorted so hard that milk came out of his nose. Which only made me laugh more. By the time breakfast was over, Mum had managed to coax Billy out from his cornflakes fort, and I'd forgotten all about the cat. Almost.

"You'd best get to school," Mum said as she cleared the table with a clatter and clang. "Don't want to be late."

Billy looked down at his lap and fidgeted.

"I don't think I can go," he said.

"Why not?" Mum said.

"I don't feel well. I think its dengue fever."

Billy hates school, so he's always inventing new illnesses to keep him off for a day. That year he had already used up his excuses of colds, flu, headaches and even a bad case of the runs, so he had been getting creative. Dengue fever had been mentioned on the nature programme we'd watched last night.

"I don't remember us trekking through any jungles lately," Mum said gently.

"The grass is the garden is getting pretty long," Billy mumbled.

Mum put her hand on his head.

"No fever," Mum said. She tickled him under his arm and Billy yelped and flew off his chair. "Reflexes good too. I think you're cleared for school."

Billy scowled, pulled on his backpack and stormed out the door. He let it slam behind him, leaving the whole house rattling. Mum sighed.

"Will you talk to him about at least trying to make some friends?" she said. "I really want him to have a better time in this school than the last one."

As we walked towards the school, I tried to think of the right thing to say. Billy had changed schools four times and he still hadn't figured out how to fit in.

"Listen," I said at last. "You have to think of school like a jungle. The teachers are the elephants. They watch over everything and hang out at the watering hole, which is the staffroom. The older years are the lions. They have been there so long that they basically own everything. Then there's the bears, which are the footballers, no one messes with them. And the monkeys, which are the popular girls, they're annoying and always chattering and grooming themselves. And then, well, there's everyone else: zebras, meerkats and antelopes. And even though lions and bears can eat the other animals, everyone's fine as long as they're part of a pack."

Billy looked up at me, confused.

"You just need to make some friends," I finished.

Billy scowled again. He didn't like big groups of people and he hated talking to strangers. Which made it hard to make friends. The shiny mermaid scale backpack he insisted on wearing didn't help much either.

"Look," I tried again. "We're not like other

people. We need to fit in. We can't draw attention to ourselves. What if someone started asking questions? What if someone found out about us?"

I didn't really think that would happen. For one thing, I knew that no would believe the truth. That we were cursed. One time the kind nurse at my first school had asked me why I got so many stomach aches and I told her about the curse. She'd just patted me on the head and given me some Calpol.

"But what if I try to make friends and then no one ends up liking me anyway?" Billy said in a tiny voice.

"I like you," I said. "So they will too."

"That's because you're my brother. You have to like me," Billy said.

"Fine, I don't like you then, you suck," I said, playfully punching Billy's shoulder.

"Shut up!" Billy laughed.

But as we turned the corner and our school came into view, Billy's face fell.

"I really don't want to go to school," he said.

"I know, but just close your eyes and think of one good thing to get you through today," I said. "There must be one."

Billy closed his eyes, took a deep breath and then smiled.

"We're going to the aquarium next week," he said

at last. "And horrible Davy and Jess are already daring each other to touch the stingrays. Maybe one of them will get electrocuted and die."

"We can only hope," I said as we reached the school gates.

St Jude's was one big school, separated into two buildings. The smaller new building was the junior school, whilst the imposing red brick building was the secondary school. It was another thing I liked about living in this town. I could walk Billy to school and back.

"Hey, it's Neena," Billy shouted, and waved.

I groaned. Neena was the Kapoor's daughter. She lived across the street from us. And always had her bedroom light on. It was her window that had been lit up the night we moved in. One night in my room I had caught her staring at me through the window. I'd waved, but Neena had ducked out of sight. I'd thought about how the crystal jellyfish lights up to say hello. So I had clicked the light on and off and after a moment Neena had copied. We'd done it nearly every night that first week. It was like having a friend in the dark. I was sure we would become best friends at school, but when I started, I realized that wasn't going to happen. The other kids looked at her like she was something horrible like a stink beetle or a grub. Nobody was friends with her and if I wanted to fit in, I couldn't be either. So I tried to avoid her. But it was hard not to stop and stare when I saw her. Because Neena was like nobody I had ever met. She wore a bright red coat that looked like a cape and silver sparkly Dr. Martens that got her into trouble at school almost every day. That's when she wasn't being told off for reading detective books in class. Old books with titles like:

*How to Get Away with Murder.*

*The A-Z of Poisons.*

*Deadly Deaths and Poisonous Plots Through the Ages.*

Another thing that made Neena noticeable was that everywhere she went, her parents followed. Not right into the classroom, but they walked her to and from school every day. Now she was striding across the street, looking like she was trying to pretend her parents weren't two steps behind her. She glanced up from her book and then she stopped and stared at something. Something behind us. I turned to look, and a nasty feeling crept over me. It was a black cat.

# CHAPTER 4

I was still worrying about the cat when I got into registration. I'd spent a good ten minutes checking to see if it was still following me. But it was gone. I tried to convince myself it was just a coincidence. Or a different cat altogether. But I couldn't get its big yellow eyes out of my head. I was still thinking about it when I saw Jackson, Dylan and Liam waving me over from the back of the classroom.

"All right, lads," I said as I pushed the worry down into the pit of my stomach.

"You missed the register, but we totally covered for you by saying you were in the bog," Dylan said, adding, "With the squits."

"Thanks, I think," I said.

"What are friends for?" Jackson said, making a fart noise with his armpit.

Our form tutor, Mr Townsend, looked up crossly from his register. Jackson pointed at me.

"Stomach still bothering you, Mr Bradley?" he said, and the girls in front of us giggled.

I rolled my eyes at Jackson, but I couldn't stay mad at any of my friends for too long. They were the reason I loved St Jude's more than any other school I'd been to, and I'd been to a lot. Some of them had been really rubbish, like the school I'd gone to when we lived in Inverness. It was always cold, and the PE teacher made us go on long runs in the rain. Or the high school I'd gone to when we'd lived in our trailer in Cornwall. You had to ask permission to take your jumper off, even when it was the middle of summer. And you got points taken off you if you had to go to the loo during class. But the very worst had been the huge primary school in Wales where everyone picked on me. Daniel Starks had nicknamed me "Moon Head" and even invented a game where you got points if you hit the back of my head with a rubber. I'd sit right up front by the teacher in class and hide in the loo or the car park in between lessons. But Daniel found other ways to get to me. He broke into my locker and put all my stuff in weird places. The gloves Mum had knitted for me ended up in the tadpole tank. My PE shorts got pinned up to the classroom door, with the tag pulled out and the size ringed in highlighter. So, when our teacher asked whose they were, I was too embarrassed to own up. In the end, when the curse caught up with us and our caravan blew away, I hadn't been sorry. After that, I started learning how to fit in. Learning the rules of the jungle. What to do and not do in order to blend in. So in one school I joined the rugby team and hung out with the jocks. In the school after that, they didn't play rugby, but they did have a big drama department, so I did after-school plays with a group of girls. In my very last school, Millburn Academy, they didn't do sports or have a theatre, so I focused on getting good grades and hanging out with the smart kids. I'd managed to fit into nearly all my schools so well that I'd always been invisible. Just another one of the herd.

Until I met Jackson. Jackson was tall and good-looking and his dad was the manager of the local football team, the Hockley Rangers, and had even played for Newcastle United once. This made Jackson the most popular boy in our year, if not the whole school. Liam and Dylan were also cool. Liam was really into art and was always changing his hair; he'd had an afro, short hair with patterns shaved into the sides, and one holiday he even dyed it blue.

And Dylan could make the whole school laugh with his impressions of our teachers. With them, I was no longer invisible. I was *popular*. Which was more than I could say for Neena Kapoor. I watched her get bumped and tripped up on her way to history class. She put her chin up like she didn't care, but I knew that she did. I wanted to tell her if she just tried a bit harder, or wasn't quite so odd, she wouldn't get half as much hassle.

"Did you manage to get our project finished?" Liam asked.

"Yeah," I said. From my bag, I took out the Ancient Egypt project that we'd spent all last term making.

Mum had taken me to a printer shop next to her work and her friend there had helped us make it into a proper book. It had a brown leather cover and *The Curse of the Pharaohs* printed on it in gold lettering.

"This is amazing!" Dylan said, grabbing it out of my hands.

"It looks like a book from *Indiana Jones*," Jackson said, flicking through all the pages and pictures we'd drawn together.

Last term we'd had to get into groups and pick a project about Ancient Egypt. I was the one who said we should do ours on the Curse of the Pharaohs. I figured I was a bit of an expert on curses, after all. I'd got into it a bit more than either Dylan or Jackson and Liam. In fact, I'd spent most of half-term on it.

"Yeah, this looks proper good," Liam said, flicking over an Ancient Egyptian map I'd drawn on paper stained with tea to make it look like papyrus.

"Do you think it's enough to win Miss Ackerly's cup?" I asked.

But Liam had already lost interest. He was staring at the phone he'd managed to smuggle past Mr Townsend. When we first started this project, he'd been really excited. He wanted to know all about curses. I had even wondered whether one day I might tell him about mine. We'd been close for a while. We'd hung out in his attic, which was filled with all these garden gnomes his older brother had nicked from people's houses, and told each other secrets. Just stupid things, like he'd told me about not being able to swim and I'd told him about how I hadn't been able to ride a bike until I was ten. But since Liam's mum had got sick, I hadn't gone around his house and Liam didn't seem to care about pharaohs, curses or even secrets. He spent most of his time now checking his phone. Despite his indifference I couldn't help feeling excited. I'd never won anything I cared about before. I'd been part of clubs and groups, but only ever to fit in. This project was the first thing I'd done that I was proud of. I couldn't wait to tell Dad about the cup. I was hoping it would make him realize that, despite the curse, I had a lot going for me. And then maybe he wouldn't look at me with such a sad face any more.

Miss Ackerly wasn't in our history classroom when we arrived. That was weird because she was usually waiting for us.

Liam sprawled out on the back table and Jackson and Dylan grabbed some chairs to sit next to him. I liked Dylan nearly as much as Liam. Dylan was not only funny, but he was also super smart; he knew the answer for nearly everything. He was even preparing to go on *Junior Mastermind*. But Jackson was the special one. Head of the year eight football team, a prefect, and he always had the latest of everything, phone, headphones, trainers, you name it. Despite all this, he could be a bit mean. Now, he was flicking bits of Blu-Tack at Neena's back. She was hunched over another one of her weird detective books, and her long black plait hung neatly over the back of her chair. I was secretly relieved when the classroom door opened and suddenly everyone was on their best behaviour. Then I saw that it wasn't Miss Ackerly stepping through the door; it was Mr Anson.

Mr Anson had been a proper teacher once, maybe

back in the 1800s, but now only came back to school to do supply teaching. He always trailed off before finishing a sentence, so nobody ever knew what he was talking about. His lessons were terrible and the perfect excuse to mess about.

But for once I wasn't looking forward to an hour off. I had waited weeks to hand in my project to Miss Ackerly.

As soon as the class saw Mr Anson, everyone began preparing to relax. People moved chairs and pushed desks together so they could sit in big friendship groups. The only person who didn't move was Neena. She got out all her notebooks, pens and pencils. Before she zipped up her bag I saw inside; there was a torch, a spare pair of clothes, a multipack of Hula Hoops, a flask and a sleeping bag. I wondered if Neena was going to a sleepover. Although I couldn't think who would invite her. The bag reminded me of my own one, which I kept under my bed. A middle-of-the-night getaway bag. Neena snapped her bag shut. Mr Anson cleared his throat.

"Miss Ackerly is taking a short leave of absence..." he began.

"Where's she gone?" I asked.

"Is she ill?" Dylan added.

"Is it something catching?" asked Jackson.

But Mr Anson ignored us and carried on.

"While she is off, we're going to do a project on family trees. Take a sheet and pass it—" Mr Anson flicked his wrist lazily to indicate the person to the left of us.

"On the sheet you'll see spaces for you, your immediate family, grandparents and, uh, other relatives. Fill in as much information as you can."

We all looked at him blankly. He sighed and continued.

"Start with the basics. Your name, age, where you were born and such and such. Then fill in as much as you can about your close family – mum, dad and grandparents. There's homework too."

We all groaned.

"Your homework is to find out more about your extended family. That means grandparents, great-grandparents, uncles and aunts, cousins. Where they came from, where they lived, their profession and their personal stories." Mr Anson finished slumping down behind the desk, clearly exhausted from making so many full sentences.

Everyone groaned again. It was obviously the same lesson Mr Anson had done in every history cover class ever, so he could take a nap or read the paper. Everyone started chatting and swapping coloured pens, but I stared at the page blankly. I didn't know who my family was. Dad hadn't known his father, and his mum had died when he was a teenager. He didn't like talking about his family much. And everyone on Mum's side, the Bradley side, apart from Nana, who had died when I was little, was a mystery. The curse meant our family was scattered and constantly moving. Mum didn't even know where she'd been born. I looked over at Jackson. He was already filling his sheet out. He came from an army family, so all his family had Captain or Lieutenant Sergeant before their names. Dylan was writing about growing up in Spain and moving to Hockley when he was six. Liam was checking his phone again. I stared blankly at my piece of paper. The classroom was busy with the sound of writing and chatting. Everyone else seemed to know who they were and where they were from. Everyone, that was, except Neena. She had barely touched her chart. I caught her eye from across the room.

"Distracted by your girlfriend?" Jackson said, nudging me.

"What, murder eyes?" I said. "Give over."

It was the nickname everyone called Neena because of the books she read and also because Jackson had started a rumour about her being crazy, which was why her parents had to take her everywhere, "to make sure no unfortunate accidents happened".

"Careful. You could be next," Jackson said, humming the *Psycho* theme and waving an imaginary knife.

Dylan laughed and mimed being strangled; even Liam joined in, pretending to fall dead on the desk. I glanced back over at Neena. Even though we were talking and laughing quietly, I could tell she had heard. Her back was stiff, and she was staring straight ahead, her chin up, her hands balled into tight fists. Her knee was bouncing up and down under her desk. I felt bad then. I wanted to tell her I didn't believe the stories Jackson had made up about her and that we were all just being stupid. But I didn't – I just laughed along with my friends.

If I were an animal, I would be a chameleon. I could change into a thousand different colours to fit in wherever I wanted. But sometimes it felt like I'd forgotten what colour I was really meant to be.

# CHAPTER 5

"How was school?" Mum asked when we got home that afternoon.

"Fine," I said as I threw my backpack on to the chair and collapsed at the kitchen table.

When we had walked into the kitchen, she was hastily slipping something into a drawer. It looked like another of her mysterious letters.

"Really? Just fine? I thought you were handing in your big project today," Mum said. "Your contender for the history cup."

"Miss Ackerly is off sick," I said, taking a chocolate mini roll out of the cupboard and stuffing it in my mouth, before reaching in for another.

I caught Mum giving me a quick, anxious look.

She knew I sometimes ate more when I was upset or nervous. But this time I was eating so I didn't have to answer any more questions. I didn't want to talk about school. I still felt bad about making fun of Neena today. Even if it was something I had to do to fit in. I knew if I told Billy or Mum about it, they wouldn't understand. Mum would just give me a speech about being honest and true to myself. Which was hard to do when I wasn't sure who I am. I am Noah Bradley the popular boy, Noah Bradley the bully and Noah Bradley, the boy who's cursed.

"That's a shame," Mum said. "I know how much you were looking forward to the competition."

I shrugged and ate another mini roll, trying not to think about how small and sad Neena had looked.

"Listen, I have to go back and work at the restaurant tonight," Mum said, obviously giving up on prising any more information out of me. "Mr Armstrong is short-handed. So I'll need you to keep an eye on Billy. Is that all right?"

"Uh-huh," I mumbled.

"I've made some stew for dinner. You just need to heat it up on the stove." Mum glanced at her watch. "And hey, I've just got time to watch our show."

Our favourite show was called *Beat the Clock*. It was a quiz show where the rules got more and more complicated and hard to follow as they went on and the quiz teams always seemed to lose everything by the end. The first time we saw it, one of the contestants had a meltdown and kicked the big luminous clock until it had rolled off the stage. Mum had laughed so hard she'd got the hiccups and we'd been hooked ever since. From then on it didn't matter what kind of home we lived in or where we were, we always watched *Beat the Clock* at four p.m. on a Monday night.

For a while we even watched it all together on a little portable TV in the back of Dad's van. We'd lived in Dad's van for a couple of weeks one summer after our houseboat had caught on fire and Mum and Dad were short on money after an expensive visit to the vet for Arnold. Ferrets and houseboats are two things that shouldn't go together. But vans and ferrets are even worse. For two weeks I kept being woken up by Arnold scurrying over me. And when he wasn't, I kept worrying someone would find out we were living in a van and take us away from Mum and Dad, or worse, someone would break in whilst we were asleep. Mum tried to make us feel better by telling us it was just like camping. We toasted marshmallows on a little fire outside and she'd read us ghost stories by torch under Nana's patchwork blanket. But it was nothing like camping. Camping is meant to be a fun break away from your ordinary life; it's not meant to *be* your life. After that, whenever we moved somewhere, no matter how bad it was, I always felt relieved it wasn't the van.

That night I couldn't sleep. I kept thinking about Neena and her bag full of stuff. Surely we weren't making things so bad for her at school she would consider running away? I got up out of bed and looked out across the street. But Neena's window was dark. I flicked the light on and off, but her house stayed shadowy and still. I was too awake to go back to bed. I got out my Singapore skyline Lego set instead. It was a new one Dad had given me before he had left. I knew he had only got it for me because he felt guilty, so I hadn't wanted to open it before now. As soon as I was holding the instruction manual, I felt a wave of relief wash over me. I spread the little packets of bricks across the floor and began building.

I was halfway through building the kit when the light in Neena's window went on. It threw the shadows across my room. I got up to look in time to see another light go on in her house downstairs, just for a second, and then the whole house fell into darkness. A moment later the front door across the street opened and Neena appeared, bundled up in her red coat and fur hat. She was struggling with her duffel bag, which seemed to have grown. She began walking up the road, only turning back once to look at her house. She *was* running away. Leaving her lovely home behind, to spend a dark night somewhere alone. I thought of our time in the van, and how scared I had been. And I had been with Mum and Dad and Billy. I didn't understand; Neena was so lucky. She had a nice home in nice Verity Close with all its nice neighbours and she never had to leave. Maybe if I explained all that she wouldn't want to run away. Maybe if I apologized for school too. . .

I ran down the stairs, making a *thump-thump* sound that wasn't half as loud as the thundering of my heart. Outside the night was cool and clear.

"Neena," I cried out.

But the cold air stole my words.

"Neena," I cried out again, running after her.

"Leave me alone, Noah Bradley," Neena called back over her shoulder.

"This is mad. Running away won't make your problems go away," I called after her.

She stopped and spun around, her eyes blazing.

"What would *you* know about problems, Noah Bradley? You're one of the most popular boys in school. Everything is easy for you, isn't it? You don't have a clue what it's like to be alone, or different, or to have no one to talk to."

But I did know. I knew better than anyone.

"Look, I'm sorry I've been such a jerk to you at school. . ." I began.

But Neena wasn't looking at me any more. She was looking at the sky, and I saw her mouth grow wide in shock. There was a shriek, a terrible shriek. But it didn't come from Neena and didn't come from me. It came from the sky and it echoed all around us. Then I heard it. The sound that haunted my dreams. The sound that woke me up at night. The sound that chased us from home to home.

*Whoosh, whoosh, whoosh.*

The beating of a thousand dark wings.

# CHAPTER 6

A large shadow crossed the moon and then the stars disappeared from the sky.

"Neena, come on – we have to run!" I yelled over the thundering sound.

But Neena had pulled a torch out of her bag. She wanted to see what was coming, just like I had the first time I'd seen them with Nana. That time the birds had torn me out of her arms. She had managed to rescue me, but I could still remember their black feathery wings, darkness and pain.

"We have to go!" I yelled.

Neena was standing tall in the middle of the street, pointing the torch high.

*Click.*

The torch lit a narrow beam across the street. The tops of the trees began to shake in every garden, their leaves scattering along the street. And all the while the *whoosh whoosh whoosh* sound grew louder. The hair on the back of my neck rose up. My fingertips prickled. The air was filled with static. My heart pounded and my breath came in thin ragged bursts. I looked back at my open front door. I could make it if I ran. But Neena was still standing in the street with a frozen look on her face, the torch shaking in her hands.

"What's happening?" she called out. The birds' awful shrill shriek echoed around us once again.

"Neena, run!" I yelled, bolting across the street and grabbing her arm.

But it was too late. The birds were on us. Neena fell to the ground, the torch spinning across the street, catching the shadows of wings and beaks and raised talons. Neena screamed. But her scream was drowned out by the screech of birds. I tried to fend off talons and beaks. A beak scratched deep into the back of my neck. A talon raked across my ear. The sleeve of my pyjamas was ripped open and I felt a sharp sear of pain up my arm. Neena cried out again as two birds wrestled with her plait. She pulled her hood up to protect her face. But it was torn from her coat and flew like a flag high into the sky, scattering the birds for just a moment. It was enough time for me and Neena to make a break for it.

"Over there," I said, spotting a reflective strip of the barriers over some fresh building work that had been started on the pavement. There was a trench behind them. "Go," I yelled, pushing Neena ahead of me.

We rolled and tumbled under the barriers and into the ditch along the side of the road. The birds swooped over us, the soft velvet tips of their wings brushing past my face. I buried my head into the gravel and squeezed my eyes shut as they passed over. My heart pounded. My hands shook. I could feel blood drip from the back of my neck. But everything was still.

"Are they gone?" Neena breathed out.

I swallowed back the fear I felt and peered over the trench. The sky was clear. The street lights flickered back into life. But as the sun started to climb in the sky I could see the dark shadow of the birds on the horizon. They were circling back.

*Always get to shelter* – that was what Nana would say. I eyed my open front door. The light was on in the hallway. A pinprick in the dark. It felt a thousand miles away. But we had to make a dash for it. We weren't safe here.

"Neena, on the count of three we need to run."

"What?" Neena gasped.

"One," I called out, grabbing Neena under the armpit.

"Two," I said as the trees began to tremble.

"Three," I said as a deafening screech filled the air.

"Run!" I shouted as the sky turned black.

Neena was already on her feet and we were flying across the road. The open door of my house was getting closer and closer. I could feel wings beating down on us. We were through the garden gate, then the doorway. We tumbled into the hallway. My hands and knees slapped on to the cold, hard tiles. But we weren't safe yet. The air was thick with the cries of the black birds from the north.

"The door!" Neena yelled.

I staggered to my feet and slammed it closed behind us, just in time.

*Thud.*

*Thud.*

*Thud.*

The birds crashed into the door, the walls, the windows around us. The house shuddered. I held my breath and hoped for what felt like the thousandth time that Mum was right, that the house had old bones and that would protect us. There was a horrible screech. And then, silence. Neena crouched on the floor, her hands covering her head. I could hear her breathing, hard and fast, but nothing else.

"Is it over?" Neena asked, looking up tentatively.

I peered through the window. The street lights had flickered back into life. There were small, dark shapes lying on the street and I shuddered. Dead birds.

"I think we're safe now," I said.

"What were they?"

"Birds," I said.

"Those were not normal birds," Neena whispered. "What's going on, Noah? What are you hiding?"

In the dim hallway, all I could see was the whites of Neena's eyes. In the dark it would have been so easy to tell her everything. About the curse that followed us. About always having to run in the middle of the night to some faraway place. About how we would have to do it again, now that the birds had come. That no matter how well I managed to fit in, there was always a part of me that felt different. Somehow, I knew Neena would understand the last part. But I knew all the trouble I could cause if I told someone the truth.

So instead I said: "You want to talk about hiding things? You were the one sneaking out at in the dead of night, with a bag packed."

The fear in Neena's face dropped away, and her mouth formed a thin angry line.

"You had no right to spy on me," she hissed.

"Where were you going?" I asked.

"That's none of your business, Noah Bradley," Neena said.

"Fine. Then neither is this," I replied, folding my scratched arms.

Neena opened mouth. I could tell she had so many questions.

"Fine," Neena said, flicking back her thick dark ponytail. "It looks like we both have a secret to keep."

I watched Neena creep cautiously back to her house. She picked up the bag that had been torn from her hands and cradled it to her chest a moment, before closing her front door behind her with a bang that I heard across the street.

I went upstairs and checked in on Billy. Arnold was squeaking madly in his cage, but Billy was sound asleep, his chest rising and falling under his duvet cover, his foot poking out of the end of the bed. Billy could sleep through hurricanes, earthquakes and twisters. I gently popped his foot back under the covers, before picking up Arnold and heading back to my room.

Tomorrow I would have to tell Mum what happened, and we'd have to move all over again. I'd never get a chance to make things right with Neena or say goodbye to my friends or win the history prize. I'd never get to be normal.

I looked at the Lego Singapore skyline I'd nearly finished building and then, suddenly, kicked it down. The plastic bricks cut into my feet, but I didn't care. I knocked the rest of the models from the shelf. Even the little Lego village that me and Dad had built together. Then I pulled out my worn-out suitcase from under the bed and began tossing everything into it. Books, clothes, games. I stopped when I got to my school uniform. I smoothed my hand over the yellow-and-turquoise striped tie. I couldn't bear to pack it away.

So instead I pulled out Nana's blanket and snuggled into it. I hid under the patchwork panels, on to which were sewn pictures of the house in the woods, the foxes and the owls and the magical objects that once kept my family safe. And I hoped for the hundredth time that all the love and magic woven into its stitches would fix everything.

# CHAPTER 7

I woke to the sound of our doorbell. I heard Mum's bedroom door open and her footsteps down the stairs, her opening the door and the sound of a friendly voice. The post, perhaps, although it was a bit early.

She would have seen the dead birds in the front garden, I thought. At any moment she would come running up the stairs, burst into my room and tell me that we had to move. Then we would have to start shoving all our neat new life into bin bags and leave Verity Close for ever.

I lay in bed, listening to the house, clinging on to normality for just a bit longer. The hum of the refrigerator, the wind howling along the alleyway, Billy's snoring across the hallway. Arnold nibbled at my ear.

"Just a bit longer, just a little bit longer," I said to him stroking his soft cinnamon fur.

Arnold ignored me and slid into the arm of my pyjamas.

"Fine, fine, I'll get up," I told him. I pushed back the covers. I looked around at my perfect bedroom. The one that had my own bed, and all my own things. The one that I had painted with both Mum and Dad. I felt my heart break at the thought of leaving it.

I slipped out of my room, Arnold wrapped around my shoulders and headed down the stairs. I made sure to land on every creaky part, so I would remember just how they felt. I didn't know when we would live in a house with staircase again.

I walked into the kitchen. Mum had her back to me. ABBA's "Dancing Queen" was belting out of the radio. I put Arnold down on the table. He squeaked happily before slipping into an open box of cornflakes.

"Mum," I said before taking a deep breath and finishing, "The birds came. They came last night."

But Mum didn't turn around. She was wiggling her bum and singing along into a wooden spoon,

"*Dancing queen, feel the beat of the tangerine,*" she sang.

It was how Billy sang the song. He was always getting lyrics mixed up, even with his hearing aids in.

So Mum, Dad and me would join in so he didn't get upset. I couldn't hear any of the songs from our car trips with anything but our made-up lyrics.

"Oh, Noah," Mum said, jumping. "I didn't see you." There was a stack of pizza boxes next to her.

"What are you doing?"

She threw open the lid and the smell of melted cheese filled the room.

"Before you say anything, I don't think we give pizza as a breakfast food enough of a try. And technically this is my dinner anyway..."

I stared at the pizza. *She hasn't seen the birds*, I thought. *She still thinks everything is fine.*

She came over and rubbed my arm.

"I know you wanted to win that prize at school. But your project was still the best. And I know how hard you worked and that shouldn't go unrewarded. So, I got your favourite."

"All the toppings, no cheese?"

"All the toppings, no cheese, you weirdo," Mum said, opening another box covered in pineapple, sausage, peppers, olives, pepperoni and silvery anchovies on top of a layer of shiny tomato sauce.

I took a piece and nibbled on the end. But for once I wasn't hungry; I could still hear the screech of birds, feel their sharp black wings closing over me. I glanced at Mum, who was eating pizza and humming along to the radio. Had she really not seen the bodies of the birds? Maybe the rain had washed them into the gutter. Maybe she had been too tired to notice. Maybe I had just dreamed everything. But I could see scratches, red and raised on my arm. I pulled my pyjama sleeve down.

"And I've got something to celebrate too," Mum said.

"Pizza, the best of all breakfast foods," Billy said, emerging sleepy-eyed at the kitchen door.

"And did my little prince sleep well?" Mum asked Billy, reaching out to give him a hug.

"Mu–um," Billy said, wriggling away from her.

Billy had finally got to the stage where he hated people hugging him or holding his hand.

"Well, did you?" Mum said.

I could feel Billy stiffen. I had been sure he had slept through everything last night, but he paused from devouring his pizza and gave me the smallest, saddest look. He knew. The question hung in the air. It was like the kitchen was frozen. I imagined the frost moving across the window, spreading out over the kitchen table, creeping up our legs. I wanted to hold this picture in my head for ever. A family eating pizza for breakfast, celebrating my history project and

Mum's good news that was to come, ABBA playing on the radio. I knew as soon as I opened my mouth, the ice would break, and our world would be shattered once again.

"Mum," I started, and then the kettle whined.

"Can't have breakfast pizza without coffee," Mum said, bouncing up from the table.

She tipped some beans into our little coffee grinder. I could feel myself shaking. My throat was dry, but I had to try again.

"The birds came," I said, speaking very fast. "Last night. They attacked me and Neena in the street."

The coffee grinder roared into life and drowned out my words. The rich warm smell of coffee filled the little kitchen. Mum turned around, smiling. She hadn't heard a word. Or at least she was acting like she hadn't.

"How many times do I have to tell you – ferrets don't belong on the breakfast table," Mum said, moving Arnold into Billy's lap and placing three of our best chipped china cups down.

"Now. I propose a toast. To my brilliant son for his amazing project. And to his amazing mum –" she grinned widely "– who just got promoted to assistant manager of the Fat Olive."

"Yay, more free food!" Billy said.

I kicked him under the table.

"And also, really well done, Mum," he added, rubbing his shin.

Arnold made a funny little squeaking sound from Billy's lap and Billy picked him up and put him to his ear and nodded, like Arnold was telling him something very important.

"Arnold thinks you're going to be running your own restaurant in no time. He just hopes it allows ferrets at the table."

"I don't know about running my own place," Mum said. Her face was flushed and happy. "But this is certainly a step in the right direction."

Mum's dream had always been to have her own restaurant. This was the closest she had ever got. She's had to take so many bad jobs. A portable toilet deliverer, a credit card telephone salesperson, a funeral director's assistant. She glanced over at me.

"You're awfully quiet, Noah. Is everything OK?"

I ran my finger around the gold rim of the special china cups Mum had got in the local charity shop. We hadn't drunk out of them since the first day we moved in. Before Dad left. Before the birds came. Back when I was happy. That was when I decided: I would give us one last day. One last day to be happy. To pretend we were a normal family. It couldn't hurt. Could it?

"It's really great, Mum," I said. "You are going to make an amazing assistant manager!"

Mum smiled, one of her full-beam ones that made her light up.

"Thank you, Noah," she said. She glanced at the clock. "You two had better get going. Take the pizza boxes out, would you?"

Outside, dew was settling on the rose bushes, and Mr Kapoor was picking up his morning paper. Cautiously, I looked up and down the street. There was no sign of what had happened last night. Or at least, almost no sign. I saw it lying stiff and still on the windowsill. A single black bird. I wondered if the foxes had taken the others. I picked up the bird, folded its wings gently and laid its beak softly on to its feathery belly. I stroked the iridescent feathers, before pushing it deep into the rubbish bin.

# CHAPTER 8

I only meant to keep it secret for one day – one day, so that we could all be happy.

And then it was another day because I wanted to apologize to Neena. I had been mean, and I wanted to make things right before I left. But Neena didn't come to school the rest of the week.

And then Billy had his class trip to the sea life centre. Billy had never been on a class trip. He'd missed a lot of school when he was younger because he'd been sick and then there had been all his hearing complications; that, on top of all the moving, meant he missed all the things eight-year-olds should get to do. Like birthday parties with friends, school discos and sleepovers. Sometimes I worried that if Billy didn't get used to being around other people his best friend would always be Arnold the ferret. So I wanted him to go to that. And then it was the weekend. And I thought it couldn't hurt to just have one more weekend with my friends. On Monday, I told myself, I would tell Mum everything.

So on Saturday morning when Jackson, Dylan and Liam called for me, I acted like everything was fine.

"Where do you want to go?" Liam asked, wheeling his bike next to mine.

"Let's go up Baxter Hill and look for old Saxon and Viking things," I said. "Buried treasure."

I'd spent all morning planning the weekend out. I was going to do all my favourite things with my friends. Play football in the park until we were covered in mud, buy bags of sweets from the weird-smelling corner shop and sneak into the cinema to re-watch the exciting bit of the new superhero movie. But first I wanted to go to Baxter Hill. One of the places that Mum had pointed out on our A–Z map on our second night at Verity house.

"This is the largest hill in the north," she had said. "We can go sledging in the winter. And in the summer, we can go mountain biking. Or hunting for Saxon treasure."

There was a picture online of a Saxon horde found

on the hill. I liked the idea of finding something like a dagger or a helmet or even just a gold coin. I imagined a picture of myself in a newspaper.

*Noah Bradley, 12, Finds Long-Lost Treasure.*

Then I'd donate it to a big museum so I could have a little plaque with my name on it. Something that thousands of people would see. We hardly stayed anywhere long enough for people to remember my name. But if I found something and gave it to a museum, I wouldn't be forgotten. And it would be something me, Jackson, Dylan and Liam could share for ever. They wouldn't be able to forget me, even after I left.

Jackson rolled his eyes.

"Buried treasure? What are we, eight?"

I felt my face get all hot.

"We could look for treasure first, and then race our bikes down the hill?" Liam said, shooting me a small smile.

"Yeah, all right. We can see how fast my bike is," Jackson said.

Jackson's dad had just given him a brand-new limited-edition BMX. He been showing everyone pictures all week and now he was popping wheelies and twirling the handlebars.

"I heard a boy from year ten rode all the way down Baxter Hill without brakes," Liam said.

"I heard he ended up in a tree," Dylan said.

"I heard his brain exploded from the speed," I added.

Jackson and Dylan groaned and nudged me into the road.

"We could set a new record," Liam said, sounding excited for the first time in ages.

"The fastest anyone has ridden downhill is 167 kph," Dylan said. Dylan knew all sorts of sports facts. He was like a walking encyclopaedia.

"So how long would it take?" Liam asked again.

"I dunno. My sister said she did it in ten minutes," Dylan added.

"My bike could do it in half that," I said.

Jackson and Dylan laughed.

"Yeah right," Liam said, leaning over to give the back of my head a friendly slap.

"That piece of old junk would fall apart before you got halfway. Does it even have brakes?" Jackson joined in, taking his hands off his handlebars and coasting down the road.

I looked down at my bike. It didn't have twenty-two gears like Dylan's or a snakeskin design like Liam's and it wasn't as expensive as Jackson's, but Dad and I had restored it together.

We had found the frame in the shed when we moved in. It was covered in cobwebs and rust and had taken an hour to pull out from under all the old junk. Once it was out in the garden it had looked even worse. The handlebars had been bent and the rear bumper had fallen off.

"I'm sorry, Noah, it's not much," Dad said.

But I had wanted a bike so desperately I didn't mind if it was dirty and falling apart. And once Dad and I started to clean, it hadn't looked so bad. It had bright red paint and a smooth buttery leather seat and under the dirt Dad had found a French crest that made him whistle.

"That is a real racing bike," Dad said, his whole face lighting up. "Something like that deserves a second life."

Every weekend for a whole month before I'd started school, we had worked on the bike. Cleaning, fixing and polishing it. Then the weekend before my first day at St Jude's, Mum had taken me to the local bike shop, where we picked out white-and-yellow striped tape to go on the curly handlebars and white racing tyres to put on the wheels.

I'd been so excited to ride it that I'd forgotten about being nervous on my first day of school. I'd even forgotten about being careful or watching for bad omens. I'd just got on my bike and pedalled until I could hear the wheels humming and everything around me turned to a blur. I'd flown down the lane and over the hill and into the school gates until *boom* – I'd sailed straight over the handlebars and landed smack on top of the head teacher's prized Jaguar.

That was how I had met Liam, Jackson and Dylan. They had been so impressed with me leaving an enormous bottom-sized dent in Mr Hoad's hood that they'd asked me to come sit with them at lunch. I was so happy I didn't care about the huge bruise on my arm, or that I was banned from riding my bike on school grounds. I didn't even care that to fit in with them I had to pretend to like football and superheroes and not Lego and animals. Not when together we were the kings of the school.

I looked at Jackson bouncing up and down on his BMX and Dylan standing up on his bike with his arms stretched out wide, the wind blowing out his T-shirt. As I cycled side by side with Liam, I felt a lump rise in my throat. I didn't want to leave them. I didn't want to go back to being invisible.

"Last one to Baxter Hill is a loser," I called out, pedalling harder.

Verity Close went whizzing past. I could hear the

whir of my bike's wheels, the roar of the wind and the clunk of the gears shifting. I could forget about everything on my bike; the black birds from the north, Neena's sad little face in the dark and the curse that loomed over us.

I needed to tell Mum. I knew that. I would tell her everything when I got back home, I promised myself as I pedalled harder, leaving Verity Close behind.

I didn't see the darkening sky, or the foxes emerging from the shadows, and I didn't feel the first shake of the ground.

# CHAPTER 9

By the time we got to Baxter Hill it had begun to rain. The sky turned grey, then purple, then white. The light shimmered over us as we pedalled to the top. I thought of Dad up in his tower in Singapore. Sometimes he worked so high up that he was above the rain clouds. He said that everything was still and quiet at the top. I knew he'd love Baxter Hill. Up here I could see the whole city. The neat neighbourhoods, the grey city towers, the farms and parks and motorways, all laid out like Nana's patchwork quilt. I could see the red roofs of Verity Close and the wonky chimney stack of our house. If Dad was here, I thought, we could sit and talk about everything that had happened. Dad always took me to the park when he knew I was upset about something. Trying to talk to him half a world away over the phone wasn't the same. The last time he had called I hadn't known what to say and neither had Dad. We had been like two macaw parrots I'd seen at the Paris Zoo, repeating the same questions and answers back to each other.

Despite the rain, me, Liam and Dylan set off looking for a place to dig. Jackson supervized, pointing to mounds and chalk pits and generally ordering us about. But it didn't stop Liam and Dylan and me having fun. We dug up old Coke cans and bottle caps and rolled some dirty tyres that had been dumped down the hill. But after fifteen minutes of not finding swords, or crowns, or hordes of gold coins, we got bored.

"Cinema?" I said, hoping that Jackson had forgotten about racing our bikes back down.

The hill was much steeper than any of us had thought. It had taken nearly an hour to climb slowly to the top, pushing our bikes the last bit of the way up. The thought of riding back down made my stomach flip.

Jackson shook his head. "We're racing. I'm not going to miss the chance of getting the world record in, uh, in..."

"Downhill speed racing," Dylan filled in.

"Yeah," Jackson said.

He wheeled his bike closer to the edge of the hill. The hill fell away to a steep, rocky slope. The road below was filled with cars rushing by.

"Come on," Jackson said to Dylan. "If your sister could do it, so can you."

"Oh, you know what sisters are like. They make stuff up all the time. Last week she said she'd gone on a date with Andi Thomas from year eleven." Dylan laughed nervously.

"Well, we know *Noah* can't do it," Jackson said.

"Why not?" I said, puffing my chest out and sucking in my tummy. Two things that are very hard to do at the same time.

"Just look at the state of your bike," Jackson said.

"It's a classic," I said defensively.

"You mean old," Jackson laughed.

"We'll see," I said as I edged my bike closer to the edge.

The hill dropped off into an impossibly steep, narrow path before hitting the main road. Cars raced below like silvery beetles. But I shoved all the fear down to the dark pit of my stomach. I was good at that. Swallowing my feelings, and acting braver, or tougher, or stupider than I really was. If Jackson wanted me to be a daredevil, then I would be.

"All right," he said, lining his bike up next to mine and winking. "You and me, Noah?"

"Hell yeah," I said, setting my jaw firmly. "Ready?"

Liam frowned.

"Now we're up here, I'm not sure this is one of my best ideas," he said.

He flashed me a look that said to stop. But I shook my head. This was all part of the game. I just wasn't sure how it was going to end.

"On the count of three," Jackson said, and he unclenched his brakes.

"One," Dylan counted. "Two."

The hill rumbled beneath us. Jackson's bike tipped forward and he leapt off it with a yelp.

"What was that!?"

"I think the hill just shook," Liam said.

"Maybe we disturbed the Viking gods," Dylan grinned. "No boy shall ride to his doom today!" he said in a deep booming voice, pulling his jacket apart to reveal a T-shirt with Thor on it.

And even though it wasn't that funny, I burst out laughing, falling off my bike and into the wet grass. And then Dylan, Liam and even Jackson joined in.

"You guys are so stupid," Liam said, shaking his head at me and Jackson, before offering me a hand up.

Before I could take it, the ground shuddered beneath us again. It wasn't a gentle shake like before. It felt like the sky and ground were moving apart. Liam tumbled over and Jackson went flying over the side of his bike. I clung to the ground and squeezed my eyes shut.

"What's happening?" Jackson squeaked.

"Earthquake," Liam yelled back over the blare of car alarms and the birds screeching as they wheeled around in circles above us.

And all the relief I'd felt a few moments earlier drained away. Because we didn't get earthquakes in our town.

And that could only mean one thing. . .

# CHAPTER 10

I jumped to my feet. Down below, I could hear the faint wail of sirens. I caught the flash of blue and red lights and followed them along the main road, to the red roofs of our neighbourhood. But where the crocked chimney of our house should have been, a pile of smoke billowed up into the air.

"No!" I yelled, stumbling towards the blinking lights of the city below.

"Noah, what is it?" I heard Liam ask.

But I didn't stop to tell him. I threw a leg over my bike and pulled myself over the seat. I gripped the handlebars and peered into the steep drop down. But there was no time for worry. No time for panic. My family were in danger and it was all my fault.

Launching the bike high into the air, I threw myself on to the gravel path and over the edge. I could hear a gasp of surprise from behind me and then a cheer of, "Noah, Noah, Noah!"

But I didn't look back. The bike rocketed forward, it pedals spinning madly, the whir of the wheels only interrupted by the shudder and clunk of hitting a pothole. The world was a green blur of trees and grass. As the bike picked up speed, I could feel it shaking beneath me. One of the reflectors from the wheels peeled away, then the bumper rattled and flew off. I thought of the boy who had ended up in the tree. Or how Dylan said that your heads could explode from the speed. Would I explode? Would all that was left of me be my dirty old trainers? Would my bike even last that long? My mind raced with terrible thoughts. But I couldn't listen, couldn't stop. I thought of Mum in the living room, practising folding napkins into swans and peacocks, singing along to the radio and sipping tea out of Nana's gold leaf china cups. I thought of Billy upstairs trying to teach Arnold impossible tricks, like jumping through a hoop or sitting on command. I had promised Dad I would look after them. But I had seen all the warnings and I had ignored them. If anything happened to Mum or Billy, it would be all my fault. I leaned forward and pushed harder on the pedals. The

grey of the main road raced towards me. I gripped
the handlebars, held my breath and soared towards it.

I felt the full force of the road vibrating up through
the bike as I hit the tarmac. A pedal soared off as I
weaved through the oncoming traffic. Cars flew
at me, honking and swerving. My heart thumped,
my hands slipped, the bike rattled and groaned.
Everything threatened to come apart. But I couldn't
stop. Not when my family were in danger.

I veered off the main road and flew through the
pot holey high street with its tiny cinema and Indian
takeaways. Through the rain-washed side streets, full
of noisy newsagents and empty parks. Until the chain
finally broke and the bike coasted to a stop a few
streets away from my house. I could already see the red
fire trucks through the gaps in the fences. Everyone
from the neighbourhood had come out of their houses.
Some people hadn't stopped to put shoes on and stood
barefoot, gaping up at our street. I could hear a buzz
of low confused voices.

"Just one house?" I heard someone say.

"The one at the end, the one with the new
people," someone whispered back.

My heart pounded in my chest. I pushed through
the crowd, until I was at the end of my street. There
was yellow tape stretched across the road and I could

see our neighbours huddled together. Mrs Havick was muttering in Russian. And Neena and Mr and Mrs Kapoor all stood clutching one another.

"I was just there having tea. I was just there," Mrs Kapoor said. She was clutching a shopping bag so tight to her chest that the milk had leaked out all over the folds of her blue headscarf.

"I know, Anita. I know," Mr Kapoor said to his wife.

Spotting me, she looked up.

"Noah!" she said, dropping her shopping and rushing over to me.

But I ducked under her arms and darted through the crowd. I saw the bird before anything else. A large, dark one perched on the chimney. Only most of the chimney wasn't on the roof any more; it had fallen into the road. And where the front garden had been, there was a huge crater, spreading out into almost a perfect circle surrounding our house, and just our house.

And inside it, 18 Verity Close didn't look like anything I remembered. There was no bright red door, or gold curtains in the windows. It didn't even *have* windows any more. It looked like a Lego house, one without the front wall, where you could peer into each separate room. Only each room was filled with beams and bricks and smashed-up roof tiles.

"Mum!" I yelled, rushing towards the house before being caught in the firm grasp of a police officer.

"That's my house!" I cried.

"Noah, Noah!" Neena said, appearing from the crowd and ducking under a fireman's arm. "Your mum, they got her out. I saw. She's in an ambulance."

My heart thundered louder.

"Billy?" I asked.

"I don't know." Neena managed to get out before her mum pulled her away and back into the crowd.

I turned to the police officer. "My brother, he's still in there!" I said as another shudder went through the house and the last of the chimney slipped down and turned into a cloud of dust.

The little crowd around me let out a collective "ooohhh". And the police officer knelt, taking my shoulders gently and staring straight into my face. I could see he had big kind brown eyes with lots of laughter lines around them. But he wasn't laughing now. His mouth was set in a firm thin line.

"We're looking for him now. The firefighters are just shoring up the foundations to make it safe to go inside."

I could hear the firefighters calling out for Billy, but I knew Billy wouldn't reply. When he got really scared, he would take out his hearing aids and hide.

He could crawl into impossibly small spaces and stay hidden for hours. Once we had found him hidden under the kitchen sink. It had taken us half the day to find him. He had fallen asleep after eating a whole jar of peanut butter.

"But they won't know where to look," I said, panicked.

"You have to let the firefighters do their work," the officer said, taking me by the arm.

I forced myself to relax in his grip, and then, when his hold on me eased off, I tore my arm free. I flew across the street, through the crowd and the fire trucks. Finally, I ducked under police tape and down into the crater.

"Hey, stop!" I heard a firefighter yell behind me.

A streak of yellow jackets rushed towards me. But then the earth shook again, and an avalanche of bricks tumbled behind me.

Suddenly I was alone inside the house. I could hear the firefighters on the other side already pulling the wall down. But I didn't have time to wait for them. I was brave like a honey badger, I told myself, small but fearless, and I forced myself further inside. It was dark and dusty, and nothing was how I remembered it. The whole of our neat house had been turned upside down. There were broken pictures of us camping, of

Dad smiling and building our tree house, of me and Billy in our many different school uniforms spread out across the what had been our living room floor. The TV was hanging from the wall, held up only by the plug. A game show host yelled, "Are you ready to play?" as I crawled over the upturned sofa and into the kitchen.

The kitchen was worse than the living room. There was a huge crack running down the middle and every step seemed to make something shake.

"Billy?" I yelled, peering under the kitchen table.

Pans rattled around me as I shuffled through upturned chairs and broken plates. The cupboard doors swung back and forth, squeaking and banging, but there was no sign of Billy hiding behind them and no one called out. I closed my eyes. I tried to make a list in my head of all Billy's favourite hiding spots in this house.

- Under the shelf in the shed.
- In the little cubbyhole under the window seat in his room.
- In the understairs cupboard.
- In my wardrobe. He loved to hide in there and pounce out on me.

The house shuddered again, and I swallowed. I didn't have time to search them all. But just then, I heard something. A squeaky chattering sound, coming from somewhere above me. Arnold! Wherever Arnold was, Billy was bound to be too. I clambered through the kitchen and up on to the ruined staircase. I edged along the wall that was still standing, jumping over the gap where part of the staircase fell away. I fell through the door to Mum's room. The top of the house was in much better shape than the bottom. Mum's bed was still neatly made up. It was almost like nothing had happened. But dust drifted down through the lights as the house shuddered again.

I moved along the corridor and pulled open my bedroom door. Everything was just as I left it; my school uniform was hanging on the closet door, the Lego models I'd rebuilt were all neatly displayed on the shelf, the charts of animals and sea creatures still hanging over my bed. It made my heart ache looking at it. I closed the door and listened for the squeaking again. It was coming from the bathroom. I pushed open the door and there, huddled in the bathtub, were Arnold and Billy.

"You idiot!" I whispered. "What are you doing here? The whole house is about to collapse." I could feel tears running down my hot cheeks.

"I went back for Arnold," Billy said. "He doesn't like loud noises, or the dark."

"Shall we get out of here?" I said, putting my arm out, only for Arnold to race up it and curl safely around my neck, nibbling at my ear. I pulled Billy out of the tub and down the staircase.

"I knew you wouldn't let anything bad happen," Billy said.

But as we headed downstairs towards the sounds of the firefighters below, I knew just how wrong Billy was. I had let something very bad happen.

# CHAPTER 11

As me and Billy and the firefighters emerged into the bright light, a wave of cheers emerged from the crowd. Neena gave a smile. Old Mrs Havick was sobbing into her shopping and Mr and Mrs Kapoor were hugging. Everyone clapped; even the police officer joined in. It was just how I imagined winning the school prize or a big game show.

But it was all wrong.

Dad had put me in charge, Dad had trusted me and now our house was in ruins, Mum was in an ambulance and Billy shook in my arms, his hair thick with dust and plaster. I closed my eyes. I wanted everything to stop, for everyone to go away, for the world to just shrink down to me and Billy, so I could hold him for ever.

We were hurried into the back of an ambulance and then everyone was asking us questions. The police officer was asking where my dad was and if we had any other family. The firefighter kept asking about our house. Did we have gas? he asked. Had there ever been any problems or reports of a leak? But all the questions made my head spin. I wanted to be like the box turtle, who could pull its head and tail into its shell and sleep up to 154 days. It wasn't until the medic in the ambulance insisted we had to be checked over that everything finally fell quiet.

"Just to check you're both OK," she said. "You look like tough nuts to me, though."

"Do Arnold first," Billy said, holding out the fidgeting ferret.

"Certainly," said the medic. "Ferret first and then you, deal?"

Billy nodded.

"I'm worried he swallowed some dust. And – I think he might have got himself a bit scared and maybe wet himself," Billy said. He bit his lip.

Both me and the medic glanced down at the damp patch on Billy's trousers.

"Well, I think your ferret has been very brave," the paramedic said, rubbing Billy's back. "And he can always have a wash if he's had a little accident."

I watched while the medic checked Billy's pulse and heart rate and looked into his eyes with a little torch. At last she smiled, looking satisfied.

"You and the ferret seem to be in perfect health. Now then, how about you, Noah?"

"I wasn't in the house when it fell down. How's my mum?" I asked, biting the inside of my lip to stop myself crying.

"She's already at the hospital. You'll see her very soon. But it's important I check you over," she said, taking my pulse. "Any pain?" she asked.

I shook my head. Everything was numb. All I could do was shiver in the back of the ambulance. The ambulance lady wrapped what looked like a space blanket over my shoulders.

"It's called shock," she said gently. "It's very normal."

But nothing about this was normal. Semi-detached houses in Hockley didn't get swallowed up by earthquakes. Just like canal boats didn't burst into flames and caravans didn't get blown off the top of hilltops. Not unless you were a Bradley. Always on the run from the shadow of the old family curse. Waiting for the black birds of the north to bring accidents and disaster. I felt so stupid thinking that it could ever be any different. I watched what was once our house get smaller and smaller, as the ambulance carried us away from the tall trees and narrow houses of Verity Close. Until finally the place we had called home was just a plume of smoke among the red rooftops.

Outside the reception area of the hospital there was a crowd of reporters. A wave of camera lights swept at us as we walked in. Billy hid behind. Hospital security kept the crowd back, but I could still hear them.

"Noah, Noah, is it true you rescued your little brother?"

"Noah, what's it like to have your house destroyed by what's being called a freak earthquake?"

Inside the hospital I could see the TV over the reception desk. It was already playing a story about us. "The Bradleys' Narrow Escape," a banner read across the bottom as a picture of our house flickered into a picture of our family. And then a picture of Mum someone had taken at the restaurant.

"Your mum is this way," the medic said, funnelling us through to a corridor reading "Critical Care Unit".

There was a big room with lots of curtained-off beds. In the bed at the end, Mum was hooked up to a lot of blinking, bleeping machines. There was a doctor with her.

"Your mum's had quite a nasty bump on the head and has broken some bones," she said. "So we've given her some pain medication that's made her quite sleepy."

"Mum," I said, taking one of Mum's hands.

It felt so cold. Her eyes flickered open and focused briefly on me and Billy. Then she let out a small sigh and closed them again.

I looked at her, all bandaged and bruised. One side of her lip was all purple and her eyes looked dark and shrunken. Her whole face was swollen like she had been stung by an enormous bee. It made my stomach sore just looking at her. I wanted to let her know how sorry I was and how much I loved her. But I didn't know where to start. In the wild, bowerbirds build amazing sculptures out of twigs, flowers and fruits to show their love. But I couldn't even say the words. All I could do was sit in the stiff blue hospital chair and hold her hand.

# CHAPTER 12

Me and Billy must have fallen asleep because the next thing I knew a tall elderly man with a shock of bright white hair was sitting at the end of Mum's bed, polishing his glasses and peering out at us through his floppy fringe. I had the strange feeling he had been watching us for some time.

"Noah Bradley," he said, licking the corner of his lip like he'd left something delicious there. "It is good to finally meet you."

"Who are you?" I said, shaking Billy awake.

"Where are my manners?" He laughed, but it wasn't a warm laugh like Dad's or even the great honking goose laugh of Mum's, that made it too embarrassing to see funny films with her. It was a small, forced sort of laugh.

"My name is Mr Grey," he said, holding out his hand. "I'm from Grey, Hardman and Hart. Accident and emergency coverage for unexpected disasters and minor incidents. Here." He held out a business card. "Take my card."

I looked at the card. It was blank, apart from the words *Mr Grey* in tiny writing in the middle. I flicked it over and a number was written in biro on the back.

"Are you . . . trying to sell us something?" I asked.

"Gracious, no," Mr Grey said, doing his stiff little laugh again. "Your mum made arrangements. In case of any accidents or unfortunate incidents, your house and family were insured. In short, if you had any accidents, we pay *you* money."

"I think you should probably be talking to my mum or dad about this," I said, handing him back the card.

"Normally, we would do that, of course," Mr Grey said. "But in these very extreme circumstances. . ." Mr Grey trailed off, looking at Mum sadly. "It is a sizeable sum, and the paperwork can take some time to process. It would be best to get it started. But as you said, I should probably wait to talk to your parents." Mr Grey picked up his big suitcase and got to his feet. "You do seem to have a lot of accidents, don't you?"

I shifted in my seat. I thought about how Mum and Dad were always fighting about money. How we never had enough. How we kept losing things we couldn't replace in every move. Maybe Dad would be pleased to find I had sorted out everything before he got back. If I could fix this, it would be a start at least.

"Wait!" I said, as Mr Grey went to open the curtain. "What would I need to do?"

Mr Grey paused.

"Oh, just answer a few simple questions," he said.

I looked at Billy, who shrugged.

"I can do that," I said.

"Wonderful," Mr Grey said, sitting back down and fishing a clipboard out from his bag. "First of all, did your family have any valuables in the house?" he asked.

I tried to think of all our precious things that had survived every move. There was Mum's wooden trunk that had been in the family for ever, my Lego kits, Arnold. But they were only valuable to us.

"There's the TV," I said finally.

"Mm-hmm. Anything else?" Mr Grey said,

polishing his glasses again. I could see his strange green eyes under the mop of greying hair, and I felt an odd sensation creep over me. Like I had seen Mr Grey somewhere before. But I couldn't put my finger on where.

"Mum had some jewellery. And some old family things," I said, thinking again of the locked trunk.

"Mm-hmm," Mr Grey murmured again, but this time I saw him grow very stiff. He stopped polishing the glasses and pushed them up his beaky nose. "And where might your mum have kept these old family things?" he asked, smiling.

Billy shifted uncomfortably beside me. I glanced at him. His fingers moved quickly, and he signed, "Stop."

"Does he not talk?" Mr Grey said, staring at Billy's hearing aids.

I hate it when people ask questions about Billy like he's not even there. I glared at Mr Grey. But he didn't flinch. He didn't even apologize. He just smiled back impassively. He was starting to give me the shivers. Maybe Billy was right. Maybe I shouldn't be answering his questions, I thought.

"So where might these old family things have been when the earthquake happened?" Mr Grey asked again.

"I'm not sure," I said.

It was the truth. Mum always put the trunk "somewhere safe". And Mum's safe place was different every time we moved.

"Think, Noah. It's very important," Mr Grey said, leaning in close.

"I don't know," I said. I lifted my eyes to his. "Actually, I think it would be better to wait for my dad to get back."

"But you're doing so well, Noah." Mr Grey smiled. "We're nearly there."

And this time when he smiled all the warmth seemed to get sucked out of the room. I noticed it had become very quiet in the ward. I could hear Mum's breathing. The beeping of the machines. And the impatient tap, tap, tapping of Mr Grey's foot on the floor.

"I think you just need your memory jogged," he said, and his hand darted inside his big suitcase.

A strange shivery feeling washed over me. And then the glass on Mum's bedside table started to rattle. Mr Grey's hand twisted again inside the bag. The hospital lights blinked. Billy caught my eye. Then he got up and started hopping from foot to foot.

"Noah, I need to go to the toilet," he said, making up an excuse to get us out of there.

"But we haven't finished our little chat," Mr Grey said.

With a great burst of sparks a light above us popped. Both me and Billy cried out in surprise.

"What's going on here?" a nurse said, snapping back the curtain.

Mr Grey smiled at her, his hand slipping out of his briefcase. "Just discussing a few insurance details," he said.

"Who are you and how did you get in?" The nurse frowned. "You can leave again, at any rate. Visiting hours are over."

Mr Grey hesitated. "It really is very important, Noah," he murmured.

"I can't help you," I said, folding my arms and staring Mr Grey in the face.

"And I said, visiting hours are over," the nurse snapped.

Another light behind us went out with a great smash. Me and Billy jumped. When we turned back, Mr Grey was gone, leaving nothing but a trail of blinking lights behind him.

"This place is falling apart," the nurse said. "I'll call for an orderly to come and sort this out." She looked at us and her face softened. "We're trying to make contact with your dad, but we haven't managed to speak to him yet. There's a very nice lady waiting for you on reception – her name is Miss Kim and she's going to make arrangements for you."

"Can we not stay?" I asked.

She shook her head.

"Not the whole night," she said gently. "Your mum would want you to get some rest. We will call with any news."

"Can we just say goodbye?" Billy asked in his small voice. "Alone?"

I looked at him in surprise. The nurse softened.

"I can give you a couple more minutes. But then you need to let your mum rest," she said.

Billy pulled the curtain around the bed.

"Mum's awake," he whispered.

"What?" I said, turning.

Mum's eyes were open. She was looking right at us.

"Noah," she said. I went closer to the bed. She moved her hand weakly on the cover and I took it. She slipped something into mine.

"It's all in there," she whispered. "You must keep it safe."

"Keep what safe?" I asked.

But Mum's eyes fluttered, and she fell back asleep.

"What did she give you?" Billy asked, his eyes

bigger than a bushbaby's.

I opened my hand. Curled like a small silver snake was Mum's necklace. The key to the trunk glinted in my palm.

# CHAPTER 13

The nurse showed us to a little room off reception to meet Miss Kim. It was the kind of room where they take people to get bad news. All big sofas and grey walls, so you don't get distracted from crying. Miss Kim was sitting at a table, her hands folded. She looked like the sort of person who got called out to emergencies a lot. She had badly brushed hair, wore an unfussy jumper, a big backpack and well-worn trainers. And around her neck was a lanyard with her social worker ID. I gave Billy a worried look. A social worker was the last thing we needed. Someone asking questions and poking into our business. Asking about all the accidents.

"Noah and Billy Bradley?" she asked brightly.

I nodded my head.

"I'm Sandra Kim and I'm here to make sure you and your family have everything you need," she said. "Now, I just need to ask you a few questions. Is that OK?"

I hunched up, folding into myself, and looked at the floor. Billy copied me. I know that if you pretend to be shy, people will give up asking you questions. Grown-ups, anyway. I spent an entire year being the shy kid at one of my schools, and learnt it made kids ask more questions about you and adults ask less.

"So, I haven't been able to reach your dad since it's quite late in Singapore. But I have left a message, explaining everything."

I nodded.

"But we need to find you and your brother a place to stay until then. Do you have any other family we can reach, Noah?"

I shook my head, thinking of my family tree assignment. For all I knew we were the last of the Bradleys. The only ones to have survived the curse.

"OK then, I've looked at the emergency contact details on your school form and one of your neighbours is listed. A Mrs Kapoor?"

"She comes around our house for tea with Mum a

lot. And her daughter, Neena, goes to our school, she's nice and has the best shoes," Billy added.

I glared at him. He was meant to be playing shy, not answering questions.

"Well, maybe she can recommend some. I could certainly do with a new pair." Sandra wriggled her feet in her scruffy trainers. "Anyway, I've talked to Mr and Mrs Kapoor and they are very happy for you and Billy to stay with them tonight. Is that all right with both of you?"

I wanted to stay with Mum. Ask her about the key. Make sure she was safe from Mr Grey. But I couldn't tell Miss Kim any of that, so I just shrugged.

"Great. Oh, I almost forgot," Sandra added, lifting a cardboard box with holes off the chair next to her. "I think this belong to you."

Arnold's nose pushed its way through one of the box's holes, his whiskers twitching as his nose sniffed the air.

"Arnold!" Billy yelped, scooping him out of the box. "Did they do a full check-up?" he asked, his face suddenly serious.

"I understand that he is in full ferret health," Sandra said, scratching his head.

"He looks hungry to me," Billy said. His own stomach grumbled. "He looks like he hasn't eaten anything all day."

"Well, I'm sure we can do something about that," Sandra said with a wink.

On the way to the Kapoors' house we stopped off at a McDonald's drive-through. After everything that had happened, the black bear in my stomach growled with hunger. I wolfed down the burger, chips, McFlurry and Billy's apple pie as well. He didn't seem to mind, as he was too busy feeding most of his chips to Arnold. I knew Mum would have told him off about that. But thinking about Mum made me feel even more awful, so I drank my milkshake and tried to forget about how bruised and pale Mum looked, or the key she had given me. The key that felt like it was burning a hole in the depths of my jeans pocket.

# CHAPTER 14

Although the fire trucks and police cars had left, half of Verity Close was still cordoned off in yellow tape.

"They've evacuated your immediate neighbours to be on the safe side. But it looks like most of the damage was just around your house's foundations," Sandra said. "You will be perfectly safe at Mr and Mrs Kapoor's," she added, opening the car door for Billy.

Sandra rang the doorbell and I could hear the tumble of footsteps downstairs and the rattle of someone in the kitchen. I wondered if Neena knew we were coming. I wondered how she would feel having me to stay in her house. But when Mrs Kapoor opened the door, Neena burst out.

"I was so worried about you," she said to Billy, wrapping her arms around him.

Billy squeaked and Neena ushered us inside. Mrs Kapoor spoke to Sandra on the doorstep.

"Such an unlikely thing to have happened. An earthquake, of all things," I heard Mrs Kapoor say.

"It isn't the first unusual accident this family have had," said Sandra, adding, "All very strange. Very strange indeed."

I tried to loiter in the hallway to listen, but Billy wanted to get Arnold into the warm. So we followed Neena into the sitting room, where I couldn't help letting out a little gasp of surprise. I'd lived in twelve different homes and everyone had looked and felt different. Nana's home had looked and smelt like Nana. All cosy chairs and warm colours and the smell of thyme and cinnamon. The houseboat that we'd lived on had belonged to an ex-navy man and been covered in medals and anchors. Our caravan, which had been used as a portable groomer, had been cat themed. It had a cat paw print welcome mat and decorative plates with cats on the walls. But Neena's house didn't look like *anyone lived here*. There were no family photos, or funny knick-knacks, or any mess. In fact, it looked more like a hotel we had stayed in once. The walls, carpet and furniture were all different shades of grey. Tasteful black-and-white pictures of landscapes hung on the wall. Even the flowers in the corner of the living room were white lilies. The only colour came from the shelf of books in the hallway, which were filled with old detective stories that Neena seemed to always have on her. I couldn't imagine someone as colourful as Neena living here. Where everything was grey and neat and felt so empty. Neena was looking at us a bit awkwardly now. I could tell she wasn't sure what she should say or do.

"It's funny," Mrs Kapoor said, finally following us in. "Your mum's been around here many times, and Neena tells me that you're best friends at school. And yet, this is the first time you've been to our home."

"Yeah, I guess that is weird," I said, shooting a look at Neena, who was looking at her shoes.

"I'm just sorry it's under such unfortunate circumstances," Mr Kapoor said, coming in with a big tray of biscuits and tea. Arnold, smelling food again, started wobbling around in Billy's box. Pressing his nose through the holes and making insistent little chirps.

"And what do we have in the box?" Mr Kapoor said.

"That's Arnold, isn't it?" Neena said, bending

down to look through the holes in the box. "He seems a bit –" Neena searched for the right words "– upset."

"You would be too if you'd been stuck in this box most of the day," Billy said.

"Well, let's see if we can find him somewhere better," Mrs Kapoor said.

"We used to have a rabbit. Thumper the magnificent. Perhaps he could sleep in his old hutch in the shed?" Neena said.

I expected Billy to argue because at home Arnold had a proper large cage he could run up and down in. But he just handed Neena Arnold's box, so I could tell his mind was on over things. Like how embarrassed he was to be wearing the horrible hospital trousers. They were too big and pooled around his ankles, and he was having to constantly pull them up.

"How about I get Billy something else to wear," Mrs Kapoor said. "We have some of Neena's old clothes in the loft."

"Thanks," Billy said. "Neena has the coolest clothes." She grinned at him.

"I've got some T-shirts you could borrow, Noah," Mr Kapoor said. "Nothing very glamorous, I'm afraid," he added, motioning to his outfit of dad shorts and baggy black T-shirt.

"That's OK," I said, wishing that we had our emergency bags with us.

They had our spare clothes, including the super-soft T-shirt Dad had given me, and Billy's glow-in-the-dark Batman pyjamas. Even in Neena's strange, perfectly tidy house, that would have made us feel at home.

"Neena, how about you offer our guest something to drink," Mrs Kapoor said, taking Billy's hand and leading him off upstairs.

Neena and her dad busied themselves pouring tea and passing me sweets and biscuits. There were pink floury cubes that smelt of roses, soft glistening doughnuts and what looked like miniature pumpkins and green flapjacks. Everything smelt delicious and even though I'd eaten nearly a whole McDonald's and felt a bit sick, I hoovered them all down.

"I'll need to do a shop," said Mr Kapoor. "Get you boys some toothbrushes and that sort of thing. You'll have to tell me what you and Billy like for breakfast, Noah."

"I can go," Neena offered.

Mr Kapoor shook his head. "It's dark, Neena."

"But Papa, it's only down the road. I can be there and back before—"

"No," Mr Kapoor said firmly. "Not after dark, you know that."

115

Neena slumped back into the big white sofa and folded her arms. I could tell this was an argument she was used to having.

We spent the rest of the evening watching TV. A rerun of *Beat the Clock* was on but it wasn't any fun without all of us screaming the answers and Mum hooting with laughter when one of the contestants threw a fit. And even though it was early, I could see Billy was falling asleep. Thankfully Mrs Kapoor could see how tired we both were and finally took us upstairs with Neena.

"You boys will sleep in Neena's room tonight," Mrs Kapoor said. "I've put clean sheets on and towels out."

We said goodnight to Mrs Kapoor on the landing.

"Sleep well, boys," she said softly, enveloping me in a warm hug. "Try not to worry about your mum. She's being taken good care of and we'll go in and see her tomorrow."

I swallowed and nodded. The thought of Mum lying all alone in hospital made my stomach hurt and my head spin. All I wanted to do was crawl into bed under the covers and pretend that this scary, horrible day hadn't happened. But Neena was still with us. I could tell her Mum had asked her to show us around and make sure we were OK. She opened the door and motioned us inside. Her room was just as grey and boring as the rest of the house. Everything was neatly stored and put away; even Neena's books were colour coordinated. I frowned. I was sure this wasn't the room I saw Neena in at night. I hadn't been able to see much through the window, but I was sure I had spotted hanging charms and walls covered in posters.

"OK," she said briskly, "light switch is over here. Bathroom is just down the hall, on the left. Do you need anything else?"

I shook my head.

"Goodnight, Billy, don't let the bedbugs bite," Neena said, giving his shoulder a squeeze. She gave me a cool glance. "Don't go through my stuff, OK?" she said, glaring at me, before clicking the light off.

Billy crawled into Neena's bed; he was wearing a pair of bear pyjamas with matching bear foot slippers that had once been Neena's. I climbed in next to him and he growled and wrapped his small arms around me in a big bear hug.

"Do you think Mum's OK?" he asked.

"I think so," I said.

"Do you think Dad will be back soon?"

"I hope so," I said.

And then there was a long pause before Billy asked, "Noah, are we safe now?"

But I didn't know how to answer that.

"Go to bed," I said, pulling the covers over him.

# CHAPTER 15

The black birds from the north had found us. They were coming down the chimney, thousands of them, filling up the house, wrapping Billy up in their dark wings. Then they were in Mum's hospital room, clustered all around her, watching her with their black eyes. Then they were chasing Dad as he leapt from building to building over the skyline of Singapore. Then Mr Grey was smiling at me, a smile that stretched right across his face. Growing wider and wider until I could see all his teeth. He was reaching into his bag and the lights arounds us began smashing. And Mum was screaming, "Keep it safe! Whatever you do, keep it safe!"

I woke with a jolt, wrestling with the blankets.

My heart thumped and my T-shirt was wet through. It took me a moment to realize I wasn't in my own room. Everything that had happened came flooding back. The birds, the earthquake, Mum in hospital. The strange man, Mr Grey. The key that Mum had pressed into my hand. I lay awake, listening to Billy snoring peacefully beside me. But I couldn't go back to sleep. Every time I closed my eyes, the day's events played over and over in my head like a bad horror movie.

I slipped out of bed and padded down the corridor to the bathroom. I pulled the toilet seat down and sat on the loo. Somewhere in the Kapoors' house I could hear a clock ticking away. Time was running out for us Bradleys. We would have to leave Hockley. Go somewhere new and scary. I let out a little sob and then another and another, until soon I was crying into my T-shirt.

And then the door swung open.

"Oh, sorry. You could have locked the door," Neena said, before taking a step back. "Are you crying?" she said in disbelief.

"No," I said fiercely, as I tried to wipe my face off with my T-shirt.

It was half soaked and had a big snotty mess on it where I'd blown my nose.

"Let me get you another T-shirt," she said, her voice a bit softer.

I rubbed my nose, pulled my T-shirt down and followed Neena to a room across the hall and stepped inside.

"Wow," I couldn't help saying.

It felt like all the colour and warmth of Neena's house had been trapped in this one room. Bold turquoise walls covered in maps; some I recognized, and some I didn't. They looked like made-up maps with sky cities and islands with mysterious names. Some of the maps even looked hand drawn, with pins marking important destinations. And on every surface were travel books: guides to France, Spain, Egypt, Morocco. Even the light shade was a paper planet earth and around it hung colourful glass butterflies that caught the light. They spun as I walked through, casting rainbow winged shadows all around me. It made me smile for the first time that day. And I wanted to tell Neena all the butterfly facts I knew: how most butterflies only live a week, some only days. Or how the Monarch butterfly flies thousands of miles to lay its eggs, only for the next generation to fly back to where their mothers had come from. But I didn't, I just said,

"These are amazing."

"Thanks. My sister, Jasmin, made them. She made this too," Neena said, holding up her bracelet.

It didn't look like much in comparison; it was just a string strung with a few chipped butterfly charms. But I could tell it was precious. I'd seen Neena wearing it every day at school. She didn't take it off for PE or swimming, or anything.

"I wear it every day to remind myself of her." Her brow clouded. "I'm scared of forgetting. My parents don't want to talk about her."

"Is this her room?" I asked.

"It was," Neena said. "She died."

I remembered Mum mentioning something about Neena's sister after she went on one of her coffee trips with Mrs Kapoor, but I hadn't really been paying attention. I wondered if I would have been a bit nicer to Neena at school if I had. I looked at her now, trying to find the right thing to say. But in the end all I could think of was, "I'm sorry."

"Why?" Neena said, looking at me curiously. "It's not your fault. She was in a car accident." Neena said it matter-of-factly before she handed me a T-shirt from one of the drawers under the bed.

"I'm sorr—"

"If you say you're sorry again I'll want my shirt back," Neena said.

I looked at it. It was yellow with a giant red heart on it.

I frowned at her before pulling it on. It was way too tight on me. My stomach bulged between it and the pyjama bottoms Mr Kapoor had lent me. I tugged it down and crossed my arms defensively over my belly.

"I'm not sure this is my best look," I said awkwardly.

"I think it suits you," Neena said reassuringly.

Neena being kind to me made me feel worse.

"Why are you being nice to me?" I said. "I don't deserve it. Me and my friends are horrible to you at school."

"Yeah, I guess you are," Neena said, shrugging again.

"So why do your parents think we're best friends?"

Neena sighed. "Ever since Jasmin's accident they worry about everything. They won't even let me go to the shops on my own. Or walk to school. Or go out in the dark. I didn't want them to know how bad things were at school. It would only make them worry more. So I said everything was fine and that I had loads of friends, including you."

"Oh," I said, feeling a million times worse.

"Maybe while you're here you could just pretend to be my friend," Neena added.

I looked at Neena, hunched up at the end of the bed. I thought about how kind she was to Billy. How much she seemed to care. And how both of us had things we kept hidden.

"I'd rather not pretend," I said finally. "I'd rather actually just be friends."

"*You* want to be friends?" Neena said, raising an eyebrow.

"Why not?" I said, adding a shrug like it was no big deal.

"I'll believe it when I see it," she said, grinning. "When you're with your cool gang."

I laughed. "You're so suspicious."

"Well, you haven't told me the truth, have you?" she said.

"What do you mean?" I asked.

"Come on, Noah. You can pretend to be all normal and popular and cool at school. But I know you're different. Everything about your family is different."

I stared at her, suddenly curious how she out of everyone I knew had worked that out.

"Go on," I said slowly.

Her eyes narrowed and she began ticking points off on her fingers. "There are lots of clues. You move house in the middle of the night with no moving van and hardly any luggage. Your father leaves suddenly. Then birds come out of nowhere and start attacking you. And *then* there's an earthquake in Hockley, that only destroys one house. Yours." She leaned back. "I don't have to be a detective to know that something weird is going on."

"When you say it like that... But there could be logical explanations for all of those things," I said, beginning to worry.

"Really? OK then. Explain," Neena said, folding her arms and narrowing her eyes. "Because I—" She stopped, looking over my shoulder. "Hang on a second."

She stood up and walked to the window. "I thought I saw something," she murmured.

She pressed her nose to the glass and let out a long gasp.

"Noah! There's someone going into your house!" she said.

"What?" I said, running to the window.

She was right. We held our breath as a tall, shadowy figure approached the building, and then a torch flickered on. We watched as the flashlight moved from window to window, looking for something.

I had a good idea who it was. And what they were looking for. I felt for the key around my neck.

I turned to Neena. "You want to know the truth?"

Neena nodded vigorously.

I took a deep breath.

"I have to show you something. And it's in our house and we have to get it now, before they do."

# CHAPTER 16

A few moments later, Neena, Billy and me all stood in Neena's hallway. Billy was noisily sticking and unsticking the Velcro straps of his shoes. He was spending ages getting them on perfectly straight, something he only did when he was really anxious.

"You don't have to come, Billy," I said, crouching down to look in his face. "You can just stay here."

He looked at me for a moment and swallowed hard. "I'm going with you," he said.

I knew how ashamed he felt for hiding in the bathtub and wetting his trousers. That he was doing his best to prove he could be brave. Even if he couldn't quite hide the wobble in his bottom lip.

"You sure?" I said.

Billy slapped his straps down firmly and stood up. "I know where Mum put the trunk, so you have to take me with you."

Of course Billy knew where Mum had hidden her trunk, I thought. He knew where every hiding place in the house was. "OK, but this might be dangerous. I would bet anything it's Mr Grey from the hospital who's in our house, so we need to be on guard. We might need to take him down," I said, sounding far more brave than I felt.

"How exactly are you planning to do that, Mary Poppins?" Neena said, nodding at the umbrella I was holding. I'd found it in the hallway and thought it seemed like as good a weapon as any.

"You *definitely* don't have to come," I said.

Neena bristled, but before she could reply, a light in the hallway upstairs went on. We all froze, until we heard the toilet flush and then the click of a bedroom door shut.

"We can't stand here arguing," I whispered. "Are you with me?"

Billy zipped up his hooded sweatshirt and nodded.

"Neena?" I said.

"Obviously. There's no way I'm going to miss out on the most exciting thing to happen in Verity Close."

We snuck outside, ducking behind the low brick wall of Neena's garden. The flashlight was moving across our living room. Whoever was in our house would be able to easily see us from the road.

"What's the plan then?" Neena whispered.

I looked at Billy.

"The trunk is hidden in our shed," he whispered. "Mum thought it would be safest in there, just in case anything happened to the house. So we just have to get to the back garden."

I nodded and watched the flashlight move across the front room again.

"In that case we just need to get to the side alley and then we can climb over the garden wall. We don't even need to go into the house," I said.

"We can crawl along that trench," Neena whispered, pointing at the one dug for roadworks, where we had sheltered from the birds. "That way we can stay out of sight of the house till we're at the alleyway."

"OK," I agreed, more bravely than I felt. "Let's do it." I gripped the key around my neck.

"When I say go, we run," Neena said, peeping over the wall and watching for the flashlight.

I squeezed Billy's arm.

"You OK?" I signed.

"OK," he signed back, making a circle with his thumb and forefinger.

"Go," Neena said.

All three of us ran out from behind the low wall, past the lamp post and Mrs Havick's dented VW Beetle. Billy and Neena disappeared into the trench; I was right behind them when I tripped over my untied shoelaces and went down in the middle of the road.

The flashlight stopped moving and hovered over me. I ducked down, holding my breath. The flashlight moved over me and lit up Billy and Neena, crouching in the trench. Our plan was blown. We had been seen.

"I'm going to create a distraction," I whispered. "You run for the alley."

Neena grabbed Billy's hand. Then she threw me the umbrella.

"Just in case," she said.

"Thanks," I said, catching it.

I stood up, held it up high in the air and waved it.

"Hey!" I shouted, and the torch beam jerked back on to me as I zigzagged across the road, waving the umbrella in the air.

From the corner of my eye I could see Neena and Noah sneak into the alleyway before they disappeared into the shadows. I barrelled across the road, scrambled up across the bricks and police tape, and opened the red front door of my house. I stepped inside and walked through what was left of the hallway.

There, in the skeleton remains of my front room, stood a tall, thin man.

"Hey!" I yelled, brandishing my umbrella. "You shouldn't be here, you're trespassing," I said, hoping he didn't notice the wobble in my voice.

The flashlight shone into my eyes, blinding me for an instant.

"Where is it?" a familiar voice said.

I blinked against the torchlight. Glass crunched as he came towards me. Then he grabbed the front of my T-shirt.

"I need to know where it is," he growled, pulling me close.

As the spots cleared from eyes, I could see Mr Grey's angular face caught by shadows, his thick glasses glinting in the pale light.

"I know you have it," Mr Grey said again. "If you give it to me, no one will get hurt. It's the only way to keep yourself safe." He tightened his grip on me. "Tell me."

I shivered. When snakes are afraid, they curl themselves into tight wheels. Frogs go limp. If you pick up a frog and turn it over, it will lie there with its little frog legs crossed over its chest, playing dead.

Possums collapse, start drooling, and then leak green stuff from their bum. But I wasn't a snake, or a frog, or a possum. I had to come up with a plan. I thought fast before saying, "It's upstairs. In my room."

Mr Grey nodded.

"Take me," he said, and shoved me forward.

My mind raced as we headed upstairs. It was dark aside from the torch, and the stairs were broken; I stumbled a few times, but Mr Grey moved like a cat, stealthily and never losing a step. I wasn't sure how long I would be able to fool him. I thought of Neena and Billy outside and hoped they had found the trunk. We crossed the hallway, sidestepping a hole in the landing, and I opened my bedroom door. The animal prints had fallen off the wall and on to my bed. The window was broken, and rainwater had soaked my jungle leaf curtains. But other than that, my room looked the same.

"Under the bed," I said, pointing. "There's a bag. . ."

Mr Grey knelt and pulled out my emergency duffel bag.

"Thank you," he said before eagerly unzipping it and plunging his hand in only to find the melted chocolate rolls I'd hidden in there earlier.

"What is this?" Mr Grey said, looking down at his hand.

That was when I opened the umbrella and lunged. We crashed through the door across the hallway and down the stairs. We rolled and bounced and fell down the staircase. I felt stars burst in my head and then suddenly everything went black.

"Noah," someone said. "Noah, wake up." But it sounded very far away.

I blinked. Neena was bent over me, looking worried. Mr Grey was lying flat out beside me, his eyes closed.

"Is he..." I started.

"Still breathing, just knocked out," Neena said briskly. She helped me to my feet. "Billy's outside with the trunk."

Mr Grey groaned.

"Hurry, before he wakes up."

I grabbed my duffel bag out of Mr Grey's hand, and we sped out into the street, where Billy was waiting with the trunk, looking anxious.

"Back to mine," whispered Neena, and we began to run, dragging the trunk between the three of us.

# CHAPTER 17

"OK, you really have to tell me what's going on now," Neena said.

We were in her bedroom, sitting around the trunk.

"You really want to know?" I asked uncertainly.

"After everything that's just happened, Noah, I think I deserve some answers," Neena said.

Billy looked at me, his face pale.

"We're not really going to tell, are we?" he said, drawing his legs into his chest. "What about Mum and Dad's rules?"

I thought of the Bradley rules. How the first rule was that we didn't talk about the curse to other people. How Mum had told us again and again that we had to keep it secret. That if anyone found out it could get us into trouble or worse.

But everything was different now. Mum was in hospital. Dad was in Singapore. And I was pretty sure we were already in danger.

"I think we can trust her," I said again.

Neena squeezed Billy's hand. "I promise you can," she said gently.

At last, Billy nodded.

"The first thing you need to know," I said slowly, "is that curses are real."

I opened my duffel bag and took out Nana's blanket. I spread it out on the floor. And then I began to tell the story, just like Mum did.

"A long time ago, my family followed the North Star to a strange new land," I said, pointing to the patchwork square of a boat under a big North Star.

"But our family sailed too far," I went on. "They found themselves in a wild and dangerous place, where no matter where the family tried to build a home, it was always destroyed."

Billy hopped around, pointing to the patchwork square of the sea sweeping the house away, of the wolves surrounding the house in another, and of the house being frozen solid by ice.

"What then?"

"They sought help from the strange people who lived in the hills."

"Were they witches?" Neena asked.

"Stop interrupting," Billy said.

"Sorry," Neena said, grinning.

"They weaved their magic into four gifts. A fire poker that could conjure a fire that would never go out, keeping the snow and frost at bay. A lantern that, once lit, could control the tides, protecting them from the temperamental sea. And a weathervane that could channel lightning, and once mounted on the roof, would protect a house from the mischievous stars. And finally, a door knocker that could summon owls, eagles and foxes for protection from the wolves."

"And it worked?" Neena said.

Billy scowled at her. Neena mimed zipping her mouth shut and I continued.

"Yes, it worked. But it worked too well. Our family got selfish and greedy. No longer was the small wooden house good enough. They wanted more. So they built and built until they destroyed everything, even the forest."

"And the people of the hills weren't happy about that, I'm guessing," said Neena.

"They called the black birds of the north to gather the North Wind. And the North Wind, once gentle and welcoming, turned against the family. It pulled apart the house. So each family member took one gift, before going their separate ways to follow the North Star again."

"But," Billy said, stepping in to finish, "the people from the hills do not forgive or forget so easily. They cursed the family to be rootless, chased by the birds of the north, who would bring misfortune to any place they came to call home. Until, united again with their true strength, they could bring the curse to a close."

There was a pause, and then Neena clapped enthusiastically.

"That was a pretty good story," she said.

"It's not just a story," I said. "It's the truth."

She looked at me thoughtfully. "Maybe," she said at last. "And it does explain some of the weird stuff that's happened to you. But..."

"But what?" I asked. "The story has something to do with Mum's trunk and why that man – Mr Grey – wants it so badly. He came to the hospital to find it and when that didn't work, he broke into our house. We're in danger. Do you believe *that*?"

"A good detective needs proof," Neena said. "I need to see what's inside the trunk, what that man wanted so badly. What your mum tried so desperately to protect. If everything you've told me is true. It has to be something to do with the legend."

"Mum never let us look inside," Billy said.

"So aren't you curious to know what's in there?" Neena said.

"I guess now's the time to find out," I said.

I slipped Mum's necklace off from around my neck. Shakily I put the key into the lock. But I couldn't bring myself to turn it. Whatever was inside this trunk, Mum had protected all her life, and before that Nana had. It was one of the few things that had survived every move, every disaster and every accident that had ever happened to every generation of Bradleys. No matter what catastrophe had come for us, it had never been left behind, never forgotten. Which meant whatever was inside was worth dying for.

"I don't know if I can," I said nervously.

Billy signed "Got you, brother" and put his hand over mine. Together we turned the key. There was a heavy *clunk* and we slid our hands under the lid and pulled it open.

Inside was Mum's diary, a faded photograph of a lady dancing in a green dress, and something wrapped in Nana's old yellow silk scarf. I took everything out of the trunk and unwrapped the scarf to reveal a small bronze fox door knocker. It didn't look like much, but when I picked it up, I could feel it buzzing in my hands. It felt powerful and like it belonged to me.

"Wait," Neena said excitedly. "This is an old door knocker. One of the magic objects from the story."

She stretched out a hand to touch it but I yanked it back. I didn't want to let go of it. The handle swung up and with an almost silent click fell back down. I felt it grow hot in my hands. And then from outside we could hear the foxes barking, not one or two, but dozens.

And then there was a tapping at the window.

"What's happening?" Billy said.

"I don't know," I said, shaking my head like I was coming out of a daze.

I hastily covered the brass fox up in Nana's scarf and threw it back into the trunk, banging the lid closed. For a moment everything was silent.

Then the tap, tap, tapping sound at the window grew louder.

Neena pulled back the curtains. Outside on every tree branch were owls. They were perched on rooftops and sitting on lamp posts and on the windowsill. And below them, sitting on the pavement and looking up at us, were the foxes.

"Whoa!" Neena said, snapping the curtains shut again.

"Enough *proof* for you?" I asked.

Neena nodded furiously.

"All this time," she said breathlessly, "all this time, you've been pretending to be the popular boy but really you've had a massive secret. And that massive secret is that you, Noah Bradley, are *cursed.*"

"Don't forget about me," said Billy. "I'm cursed too. All the curse going on here."

"Of course," Neena said. She sat down on the bed and looked at me. Her eyes were shining.

"Will you stop looking at me like that?" I said. "You're starting to freak me out."

"It's just impressive, that you could be such a freak and manage to hide it," Neena said, grinning.

"Thanks," I said, crossing my arms and glaring at her. "I'm glad that you find it funny that my life is a disaster. And will be for ever, because the curse is never-ending!"

"Surely not," said Neena, frowning. "What about that bit at the end of the story – *until, united once again with their true strength, they could bring the curse to a close.* Doesn't that mean the curse can be broken?"

I sighed. "I don't know what it means. None of us do," I said.

"But maybe another Bradley does?" Neena asked.

"We gave up looking for them a long time ago," I said, shaking my head.

"Mum didn't," Billy said suddenly. He was sitting in the corner, reading Mum's diary. "Look at this."

We went over and sat down next to Billy. He had the diary open, and we could see that Mum had drawn out a family tree chart just like the one we had done in boring Mr Anson's lesson. Lots of the names had *deceased* or *missing* scribbled underneath them. But our direct family tree was the most intriguing. Because Nana had a half-sister. Mum had ringed her name in red several times.

*Helga Bradley.*

Our great aunt.

Billy picked up the picture of the woman in the dress we had seen earlier. He turned it over and there was the same name scribbled on it in faded ink: *Helga Bradley, Brighton, March 1998.*

"This is her," Billy said, "and they've been writing to each other."

He pulled out a letter from the back of the slip pocket of Mum's diary. It was addressed to Mum in big, loopy handwriting. He handed it to me. With shaking hands, I unfolded the letter from Helga Bradley, the aunt I never knew I had.

"It's a reply to a letter from Mum," I said, scanning the brief lines. "From this Helga woman. She says:

*Dear Joanne,*

*I wondered when I might hear from another Bradley.*

*It has been many years and I had thought the Bradleys lost for ever. And with them, the answer to the riddle that has made our lives so restless and hard.*

*"You asked if I knew of any way to break the curse. I believe I do have an answer. And it lies, I believe, in the last part of the legend, a riddle I have always longed to solve:* Until, united again with their true strength, they could bring the curse to a close.

*The lantern, the weathervane, the poker, the door knocker. Unite those objects and restore their true power and the curse will be broken.*

*I was left the lantern, and over the years I have found the whereabouts of the poker and the weathervane. All that was lost to me was the door knocker. But now, together, we can break this curse.*

*But time is short, because there is another — one who will stop at nothing to obtain the power the Bradley objects wield. He has been chasing me. Chasing us all, I fear. So, we must meet, and soon. Let us discuss a place both safe and secret.*

*Yours, Helga Bradley."*

I lifted my eyes from the letter.

Suddenly, everything made sense. The strange letters that made Mum so excited, the arguments with Dad and why she had been convinced that 18 Verity Close could finally be our forever home.

Mum had discovered how to break the curse.

# CHAPTER 18

The next morning, just as I was sleepily coming downstairs for breakfast, the phone rang.

Mr Kapoor picked it up. "Mr Bradley!" he said. So it was Dad. They'd been trying to reach him all of yesterday.

I waited on the landing, listening. They spoke for what felt like ages. Mr Kapoor kept saying reassuring things, like, "Of course, it's a huge shock, but they're doing brilliantly," and, "We are happy to help in any way we can."

And then Mr Kapoor called for me.

"Your dad's on the phone, Noah," he called. "I'll see you in the kitchen for breakfast after."

I picked up the phone.

"Dad," I said softly.

"Noah," he said, his voice heavy with relief. "I'm so glad you're OK."

As soon as I heard Dad's voice, I felt tears prick in my eyes. I missed him. I wanted him here so badly it hurt.

"Mr Kapoor's been filling me in on what's happened. But I want to hear it from you, Noah."

I wanted to tell him everything, from start to finish. I wanted it to be like our talks in the park. Where I could pour out everything I'd shoved down into the dark pit of my stomach. But Dad felt so far away now. And I thought of the fight he'd had with Mum before he'd gone away, the one where he'd said he couldn't get his hopes raised, so I knew I couldn't tell what we had discovered last night. And that meant I couldn't tell him about Mr Grey, the door knocker, or the letter from Helga. So instead, I told him all the things he already knew, about the earthquake and Mum being in hospital and how me and Billy were getting on at Mr and Mrs Kapoor's. At the end of it, Dad was dead quiet before he eventually said, "I'm so very sorry, Noah. It's all my fault. I should never have left."

And that made me want to cry again because it wasn't really Dad's fault; it was mine, for breaking my promise. But I couldn't tell him that either. And all the secrets I was keeping made the black bear in my stomach growl and groan.

"You're coming back, though, right?" I asked nervously.

"Of course! It's just taking a little more time. There's an ash cloud stopping flights out. Everything's grounded until next week. So I've talked to Miss Kim and Mr and Mrs Kapoor and they've agreed it's all right for you to stay with them until I get back. Is that OK with you?"

"Yeah," I said. "They're nice. Neena's actually pretty OK too."

"Good. I talked to the hospital this morning. Your mum's on the mend and she's off the intensive care unit. She'll be home with you soon, they think."

And even though I felt a wave of relief wash over me, all I could ask was, "And then what? What's next?"

I knew the answer, but I wanted him to say it.

"You know what's next, Noah. We leave. Find somewhere else to live, the further away the better. It always takes the curse longer to catch up to us that way," Dad replied.

Even though he couldn't see me, I shook my head. *No*, I thought. Enough running. Mum thought she had found a way to break the curse and Helga agreed. For the first time, there was hope. There was just one thing I was worried about.

"Dad, whatever happens next, you will come back and be with us?" I asked in a small voice.

"I want to live wherever you and Billy and your mum are," Dad said. "I just forgot that for a moment."

It was settled then; if I broke the curse, we could carry on living here. Nothing would have to change, ever again.

I smiled. "OK then," I said. "Goodbye, Dad."

I bounced downstairs to the kitchen, feeling lighter than I had done in months.

"Morning, Noah," Mrs Kapoor said, her back to me, pouring out juice. "How is your dad?"

"He wants to get home," I said, pulling out a chair and sitting down.

Both Mr and Mrs Kapoor seemed to freeze. There was silence as they both stared at me.

"Noah spilled something on his top last night," Neena said at last. "So I lent him one of Jasmin's."

Then Mrs Kapoor carried on pouring juice, but all the brightness had left her face. Mr Kapoor put a hand gently on her shoulder for a moment before he said a little too cheerfully, "Well, since you and Billy will be staying here a few more days, maybe we should get you a change of outfits. Fancy a shopping trip?"

"I just really want to see Mum," I said.

I wanted to see if she was OK. But I also wanted some answers. We only had Helga's letter to go on, and I needed more. I needed to find out everything she knew about breaking the curse.

"Of course," said Mrs Kapoor. "I checked, and visiting hours are in the afternoon. So how about before we go and see her, we do a spot of clothes shopping and maybe get some ice cream. I think you could do with a treat after everything that's happened." She passed me a plate of thickly buttered toast.

I hesitated. We had a trunk upstairs full of dangerous magic and a madman on our trail. Shopping was the very last thing in the world I wanted to do. Besides, even without all that, I hated shopping. Nothing ever fit me right. And when I *did* find something I liked, it was usually too expensive.

Mum tried to make our annual shopping trips fun by finding the weirdest outfits and putting them on. She once found an outfit that made her look like a space pirate, all shiny foil, and because I had laughed so much, she had bought it. I thought of it, still hanging in Mum's closet, along with her soft fluffy jumpers and silk scarfs. And then I thought of Mum in her thin hospital gown. I wanted to make sure she would never get hurt in an accident ever again and that she had a permanent place to hang her space pirate outfit.

"Come on," Mrs Kapoor said, laying a gentle hand on mine. "We want you looking your best for your mum, so she knows you're being looked after."

I could tell Mrs Kapoor was being kind but she wasn't going to give in.

"Fine," I sighed. "Let's go shopping."

By the time we arrived at the hospital, both me and Billy were in possession of a new rucksack and two new sets of clothes. Although Billy had already dripped ice cream down his new sparkly leopard-print top.

"You know that's a girl's top, right?" I whispered at him as we sat in the waiting room.

"So?" Billy shrugged. "I like it."

"I like it too," Neena said.

Billy grinned and I rolled my eyes whilst I adjusted my new hoodie. It was purple. But it was all I could find in my size. And I was too embarrassed to ask Mr and Mrs Kapoor to buy something from the Generous Fit or Big Boy range. As I walked along the corridor to see Mum, my new matching joggers made a loud *swish, swish* sound. But I stopped caring the moment I saw Mum sitting up in bed. She looked washed out with big dark rings around her eyes, but she was smiling one of her full-on sunshine smiles.

"Mum!" I yelled, throwing myself at her, with Billy following close behind.

"Noah," Mum said, hugging us back, wincing slightly.

"Oh, sorry," I said. "Are you OK?"

"Couple of broken ribs and a bad concussion. But the doctors say I'm recovering remarkably well," Mum said. She winked at me. "They don't know how tough us Bradleys are. But enough about me; how are my best boys? Are Mr and Mrs Kapoor looking after you?"

"Yes, she brought us ice cream and got me this cool new top," Billy said.

"That woman is a treasure," Mum said. And then Mum leaned forward and whispered, "Did you manage to do what I asked?"

"Yeah." I hesitated. "But that man who was here last time, Mr Grey, he was in our house, trying to steal the trunk."

I could see Mum's breathing quicken; she gripped my wrist.

"Oh my God, Noah, what happened?" she said, her voice cracking.

"It's all right, we managed to get to it first," I said, adding, "Don't worry, we're all fine."

But Mum gripped my wrist tighter and stared at Billy, shaking her head slowly.

"I'm so sorry. I should never have asked you to get it."

"But I know why you did. It's important," I said. "And now it's safe."

"Yeah," Billy piped in. "We put it in the back of Neena's sister's wardrobe, after we summoned all the animals with the door knocker."

I glared at Billy.

"By accident," he added sheepishly.

Mum let go of my wrist. The look of worry vanished, to be replaced by a tight frown. For a moment I thought she was going to yell. But she didn't. Instead she sighed heavily and said, "Well, I did give you the key. I should have expected something like that to happen." Then she looked at us, her green eyes twinkling. "But if you looked through the trunk, you must have seen the rest. How much do you know?"

"That you were tracking down our family, because you thought they could help break the curse," I said. "And you found someone. Helga Bradley."

Mum nodded slowly.

"That's right," she said. "I posted an ad online with some of the photos I'd found of our family over the years on one of those family reconnections sites and I put our address as a way to contact us. And then one day I got a letter from Helga."

"And?" I said. I had read the letter, but I wanted to hear it from Mum.

"She said the answer lay in the last part of the legend. The riddle. *Until, united again with their true strength, they could bring the curse to a close.*"

"That's what breaks the curse?" I said. "Bringing all four objects back together?"

Mum nodded again. "I was going to write back to her and tell her we would meet. But before I could, the earthquake happened."

"But *we* could write to her," I said.

"No! It's not safe any more. Helga warned me there was someone else after them. Someone dangerous, someone who wouldn't stop. I didn't want to believe her, but she was right."

"Mr Grey," I said with a shudder as I remembered his hot breath on my neck as he'd threatened me in the darkness of our hallway.

"He's found us, and I won't do anything that could put you at risk again," she said, shaking her head miserably. "No more letters. No more trying to break the curse. It's too dangerous. Not only did I put you in the path of madman, but I got complacent. I didn't watch for the signs and an earthquake took our house.

If anything had happened to you or Billy, I would never be able to forgive myself."

Mum was shaking, but her voice was firm.

"No, things have to go back to the way they were. Watch for the signs, remember the Bradley rules; we can stay safe that way."

"But Mum," I pleaded. "If we broke the curse, we could stay here. A forever home. That's what you wanted all along."

Mum took my and Billy's hand in hers.

"There are some things that are more important than a forever home," she said. "Keeping you both safe is all that matters. And I'm asking you to stop, now, before it's too late."

All the excitement and hope I'd felt last night drained away. I opened my mouth. I tried to find the right words. Something to make Mum understand. But I knew nothing I could say would change her mind.

# CHAPTER 19

"But your mum *can't* give up," Neena gasped when I told her all about it. "She was so close to finding Helga and breaking the curse. This might be your only chance—"

"Shh," I said. "I don't want to upset Billy."

We were sitting on the bed in Jasmin's room, while Billy played with Arnold in Neena's room.

"But why?" Neena said.

"Because she thinks it's too dangerous," I said, falling back on to the bed and staring up at the ceiling.

"Parents! They always think we need protecting even when we don't," Neena said, rolling over and throwing a pillow angrily against the door. Then she sat up and looked at me. "We just have to do this on our own."

"What?" I said. "Find Helga Bradley ourselves?"

Neena looked at the closet where the trunk was hidden.

"Yes." Her eyes were shining in a way that felt familiar by now. "Your mum must have left some clues to where she is."

We both sprang out of bed and pulled the trunk out of the closet. We rummaged through the notebook. There were lists – lists of the objects, lists of Bradleys dead and gone, lists of places they had all lived. There was Helga's letter. There was the door knocker (but neither of us felt like touching *that* again). And there was the photograph. But that was all.

"OK," said Neena, sitting back on her heels. "Maybe not so many clues there. But we've only just begun. Let's try looking her up."

Neena pulled out her laptop from under the bed, turned it on, and typed *Helga Bradley* in. There were what seemed like endless search results for Helga Bradleys. After an hour of clicking through we didn't seem to have any luck finding anything.

"OK, I can see why your mum had a hard time finding your family. Bradley is a pretty common name." She sighed. "If only she'd written her address on the letter."

"But she didn't. So we're stuffed, aren't we?" I said, flopping down on to the bed and jamming my hands into my pockets.

"Not quite," Neena said thoughtfully. She was holding the photograph of Helga. "We have this."

"And how does that help?" I said. I peered at the photograph. Helga wore a bright green dress that matched her strange green eyes and a floppy hat that cast half her face into shadow. The camera had caught her mid laugh with her arms wide and one leg thrown in the air, like she was dancing. She looked full of fun and a little mysterious too.

"I have no idea," said Neena. "But Mrs Shelly the librarian might. She's brilliant at finding lost things and hard-to-get stuff. Once she tracked down a whole set of out-of-print detective novels from the sixties for me. She read them after me and always figured out who did it before the end."

"You really think she can find Helga from this photo?" I asked.

"If anyone could, it would be her," Neena said.

# CHAPTER 20

The rest of the weekend flew by, in a blur of visits to Mum and phone calls from Dad, and me and Neena having secret meetings about what we would do when we found Helga. And then it was Monday and even though I was excited to talk to Mrs Shelly, I was dreading school and seeing Jackson, Dylan and Liam.

My phone was full of texts from them, asking if I was OK and what was going on, but I hadn't answered any of them. Every time I tried, I hadn't been able to find the right words to explain what had happened. As Mr Kapoor drove us to school, my head raced with all the reasons today would be a nightmare.

1. The whole school must have known about what happened by now.

2. I was still wearing the purple hoodie and tracky pants that made me look like a human grape.

3. Billy had insisted on wearing his new leopard-print top and, even worse, had paired them with some of Neena's pink shorts.

4. My rucksack contained an ancient magical object which could summon animals. Not the ideal thing to bring to school in your lunch box. But leaving it unguarded at Neena's house with Mr Grey on the loose seemed like an even worse option.

5. I was with Neena Kapoor.

Neena had already proved herself as the best friend I'd ever had. But it didn't stop me worrying about what everyone would think when they saw us together.

My head was still racing with all my worries when Mrs Kapoor pulled up to the drop-off point. We got out of the car as a big group of girls walked past, who smirked when they saw Billy in all his pink sparkly leopard-print glory.

Neena put an arm around him and whispered, "People only stop and stare when you look truly and utterly fabulous. Look," she said, and then she twirled, her long red coat fanning out like a princess dress.

For the first time since our house had collapsed, I

saw Billy smile, and then he twirled too. The group of girls giggled and then one of them clapped.

"Aw. Isn't he sweet," one of them said.

"He's just like my little cousin," another one replied.

"See." Neena winked. "Fabulous."

But I knew no one would think I looked fabulous. I pushed my hands deep into my pockets and thought of my St Jude's uniform hanging limply inside my dark bedroom closet, covered in dust and rubble. Thankfully the bell sounded, and everyone began trudging inside.

"This is going to be the longest day ever, isn't it?" I asked.

"Just remember what we're here for," Neena said.

"To track down Helga," I said.

"That's right, so just act normal until we can find a chance to get to the library," Neena said as we reached the classroom.

"Ah, welcome back, Mr Bradley," Mr Townsend said, turning and giving me a huge grin. I'd never seen Mr Townsend so happy to see me. I'd never seen him so happy to see anyone, to be honest. He was one of these teachers who didn't always seem that happy to be a teacher. But today he was beaming. He even patted me on the back.

He cleared his throat and spoke to the rest of the class. "Now, as most of you know, Noah's house was affected by the earthquake that happened last week. And unfortunately, his house and belongings have suffered some extreme damage. Which is why he's not dressed in his uniform and is, um, dressed like. . ." Mr Townsend trailed off for a moment as he took in my very purple trackies. "Like this."

"Our Mr Bradley turns out to be a bit of hero," Mr Townsend continued, and then he lifted a newspaper. The front page showed a picture of me holding Billy outside our house. A big headline across the top read: *Local Boy Saves Brother from House Hit by Earthquake.*

"So, let's give Noah a hand," Mr Townsend finished. "To our local hero!"

Everyone in class started clapping. At the back of the class, Jackson, Liam and Dylan pounded their feet on the floor and whooped. I smiled weakly.

I sat down next to Dylan, who gave me a friendly head rub.

"What are you wearing?" he said.

"You look like James the giant plum." Jackson laughed, slapping my back.

"We've been texting you all weekend, Noah," Liam said. "We were starting to wonder if you were alive," he added dramatically.

"After we saw what happened on the news, we couldn't believe it!" Dylan said, adding, "I mean, your whole house collapsing. That's just total madness."

"Where are you even staying, Noah?" Jackson asked.

I looked over at Neena. She had told me to act normal, and normal was hanging out with Jackson, Dylan and Liam. But even as I tried to tell myself that, I felt the black bear in my stomach stir.

"Mum's friends with Mrs Kapoor, so I'm sort of staying there. . ." I tailed off, embarrassed.

"Oh my God, you're staying with psycho Neena?" Jackson said, clapping his hands like this was too good to be true. "Are you scared for your life?"

"I bet her house is filled with some proper weird stuff," Dylan added.

"Not really," I said in a small voice.

"Imagine having to worry about being murdered whilst you sleep," Jackson added.

"She's not like that," I mumbled.

But Jackson and Dylan were too busy snorting with laughter to hear me.

Liam gave me a friendly nudge. "Don't worry, Noah," he said. "I'm sure everything will get back to normal soon."

And every part of me wanted so badly to believe

it could be true. That my world wouldn't be turned upside down again. That I wouldn't find myself sitting alone, in a strange new school, waiting for the bad things to happen again.

# CHAPTER 21

At lunch I snuck off with Neena to the library. All the way there people kept coming up to me to congratulate me on rescuing Billy. Even people who had never spoken to me, including a couple of year elevens who played for the school football team. I felt like the most popular boy in school. I wanted to stay and soak it all up. But me and Neena had things to do. Relatives to find. Curses to break.

We found Mrs Shelly in the library.

"How can I help you?" Mrs Shelly said, tottering out from behind her desk on a pair of very high heels, blowing her nose. She couldn't help but remind me of a very poorly giraffe. I handed her the photograph of Helga, cautiously.

"It's for our family tree project," Neena said. "Noah's trying to track down some of his family and we were wondering if we could find out more about the woman in the picture."

"Hmm. You're not going to get too much from just a picture," Mrs Shelly said, clicking her tongue and turning the picture over in her hand. "But the interesting thing here is you have a name, a date and a place written on the back. *Helga Bradley, Brighton, March 1998.*"

"We tried looking that up alongside her name," Neena said. "But nothing came up."

"Well, that's the bit where you have to play detective," Mrs Shelly said with a big sniff. "Look for clues. She looks dressed up, doesn't she?"

I looked closely at the outfit, a shimmery green dress and hat that matched her sparkly green Bradley eyes. "Yes," I said.

"And what's she doing in the picture?" Mrs Shelly asked.

"Dancing," I said.

"And where is she?"

"Brighton," I said.

"Yes, but where exactly? Look at the building in the background," Mrs Shelly said, sneezing into her jumper.

"Brighton Pavilion," Neena said excitedly.

"Bingo. So now you have three more pieces of information. She dressed up so she's at a big formal event and she's dancing. So, it's a celebration, maybe. And it's at Brighton Pavilion in March 1998. More than enough for you to start looking for her, I think," Mrs Shelly said.

"Aren't you going to help?" Neena asked.

"What kind of detectives would you be if you let me solve it all? Plus, I need to follow up on a missing book about the Bermuda Triangle," Mrs Shelly said. She winked, before sneezing her way back to the front desk.

Neena sat down and began typing busily. "Bingo," she whispered after a few minutes. "That woman is a genius."

I leaned over to look. It was a wedding website, for the wedding of Dawn Finchley and Justin Thomas at the Brighton Pavilion in March 1998. There was a section of photographs of the wedding. After trawling through them, Neena found another of Helga. She was smiling in the background as the happy couple cut the cake. Under the photo was a list of who was in the picture. It didn't say Helga Bradley; it said Helga Ogberry.

"That's why we couldn't find her," Neena said. "She changed her name."

After we found out her name, it was easy. A quick search found an article from a small newspaper about Helga moving into an old cottage in Port Mullen.

*Port Mullen's Reclusive New Resident*

*Port Mullen, known as one of the UK's smallest seaside villages, only really sees an influx of visitors in the summer months. Residents are used to seeing them arrive by car or coach service. However, Helga Ogberry (72), caused quite a stir when she arrived by boat in the dead of night to take up residence in the abandoned Cliff Top Cottage. The old cottage, which looks over the bay, was reportedly used by pirates and smugglers in the 1800s. In recent years it has become infamous for its residents meeting untimely ends and has sadly fallen into disrepair. We tried to reach out to Helga for comment on her plans for the house but were unable to contact her. It seems Port Mullen's newest resident is wrapped in as much mystery as the old cottage.*

"This has to be her, doesn't it?" Neena asked excitedly.

The strange arrival in the dead of night. The rapidly moving into a place no one would normally choose to live in. Even her reclusiveness. It all sounded exactly like a Bradley on the run from the curse. I nodded slowly before frowning.

"This doesn't give us her address or phone number or even her email though."

"We don't need any of that. We just need to get to her. You read her letter. She wanted to meet your mum in person, for her to bring her the door knocker, so together they could break the curse."

I pulled the door knocker out of my bag and turned it over gently in my hands. I could feel it buzzing in my palm. I put it down on the desk.

"I just have to give her this and then I wouldn't have to move any more. Everything could stay the way it is," I whispered.

Neena frowned. "Well, hopefully not exactly the way it is because—" but before she could finish, Liam, Dylan and Jackson appeared at the library door.

"This is where you've been hiding! We've been looking all over for you," Jackson said.

"Come on. The year elevens want you to come play footie with them. They said we could play too. You know, with us being your best mates and all," Liam said.

"The year elevens want to play football with *me*?" I said.

I wasn't really any good at football. I wasn't even sure I liked it, to be honest. But the year eleven football team were the most popular boys in the school. They were like the lions of the animal kingdom. And they wanted me to play with them!

I looked at Neena and her firm expression and sighed.

"I can't," I said.

"Why not?" Jackson said. "What are you doing here that's so important?"

"We're working on our family tree project," I said.

"You two?" Jackson said. "Because somehow I don't think you're related," he added, looking Neena up and down and laughing.

Dylan snorted.

"And what's that?" Jackson said, pointing to the fox door knocker I'd left out on the table.

"It's a door knocker," Neena said calmly. She picked it up and held it out to Jackson. "Take a look if you want." And I could see a glint of something wicked creep into her eyes.

I felt my heart leap up into my throat. I shot Neena a desperate look. She wasn't going to do what I thought she was going to do. Was she?

"It's probably just some more of your junky rubbish. Like your pathetic butterfly bracelet,"

Jackson said, reaching over and snapping Neena's butterfly bracelet so hard that a tiny butterfly charm flew across the room. I waited for Neena to cry or scream. But Neena just stood there. Then she lifted the door knocker.

"It's time someone taught you a lesson," she said.

And before I even had the chance to get the words "Neena, please don't, no" out, I heard the soft metal click of the handle.

"What have you done?!" I roared. "Give that back to me," I said, wrestling the door knocker from her hands.

There was a moment of horrible silence before Dylan and Jackson fell about laughing.

"You had us going there for a moment, Noah," Jackson said.

"Ooooh, Neena's going to kill us all with an old door knocker," Dylan said.

Liam stood there awkwardly twisting the ends of his backpack straps and staring at the floor. But Jackson and Dylan were just getting warmed up.

"Knock, knock," Jackson spluttered.

"Who's there?" Dylan grinned.

"Neena Kapoor, the psycho freak of year eight," Jackson replied.

Jackson and Dylan doubled over again in laughter.

But they couldn't see what I could. Through the library plate glass windows, me and Neena watched as the bushes began to shake. Followed by a hoot and a growl and then a terrible haunting cry. Dylan and Jackson stopped laughing. And Liam looked up from the spot on the floor he had been staring so hard at.

"What's going on, Noah?" Liam asked.

I looked at Liam. I thought of all the times we had spent together riding our bikes, sharing our secrets, laughing at our head teacher and his ridiculous moustache. I thought of the time he had introduced me to his family as his best mate Noah. How I had eaten fish fingers and chips with his mum, brother and sister. I opened my mouth to tell him to run. But it was too late. There was a thunderous crash of glass as the windows exploded and in poured a group of thin red city foxes, followed by a deer, a huge screeching barn owl and, with the whoosh of talons and wings cutting through the air, a great big hawk. Its wings were so big that it filled the small library, blocking out the light. Neena grabbed the back of my hoodie and pulled me under the computer desk just as it glided over us. I watched from behind my hands as it dive-bombed straight for Jackson. Its talons reached down and grabbed at his hair.

"Argghhh," Jackson screamed as he flailed around, falling to the floor.

The hawk sank its claws into his trousers.

"Help me!" he yelled as there was a loud rip of material.

But both Liam and Dylan had both fled down the corridor. I could hear them screaming as a streak of red flew past us.

"Get off him," I said, throwing a glue stick at the hawk.

The hawk fluttered a moment and then, with a lazy flap of its wings, lifted itself off Jackson. Jackson scrambled to his feet and crashed through the broken library windows and off up the field, all the while still screaming and grabbing at his trousers.

"Oh, is it over?" Neena said disappointedly as we crawled out from under the tables.

But it wasn't over. Animals had spilled out into the corridor. The deer had run into the wall, chasing a teacher. Foxes snapped at the heels of year sevens. Adults were yelling, kids were screaming. Mr Townsend was trying to calm down crying year sevens. An owl crashed into a strip light and it went tumbling to the floor, narrowly missing him. Neena looked at me, her face frozen in horror.

"I didn't mean for this to happen," she stuttered.

"We have to get everyone out of here," I said, pulling the fire bell.

The fire bell seemed to snap everyone out of a panic. No one knew what to do when an owl, a deer and several foxes were chasing you. But everyone knew what to do in a fire. Teachers finally got their classes under control and began ushering them safely outside. It didn't take long before everyone was lined up in form rows on the muddy field. As Mr Townsend counted us, I glanced over at Liam and Jackson and Dylan. Liam had a huge scrape down both knees. Dylan was holding his head and Jackson had an enormous rip down the back of his trousers. Everyone could see his superhero underpants. They were all standing as far away from me as possible. From under his dark fringe Jackson glared at me. I looked down in my hand to see I was still clutching the door knocker. I stuffed it hastily into my bag. But it was all too late. They finally knew the truth. The truth was that I wasn't normal, that strange and dangerous things happened around me, and now nothing would ever be the same again.

# CHAPTER 22

I didn't speak to Neena for the rest of the day. I wouldn't even look at her. She had ruined everything. It wasn't just that Dylan, Jackson and Liam would guess the truth; soon everyone would. You couldn't keep anything secret in a school. There would be whispers and then the rumours and then having to sit alone, or worse, finding my PE kit in the toilets or hanging on the whiteboard. People didn't like strangeness, or things they couldn't understand. All those years of blending in, acting normal. And Neena had ruined everything.

When Mr and Mrs Kapoor came to pick us up after school, I got into the car without saying a word. Billy didn't seem to notice. As soon as he bundled his way into the back of the Mini, he started going on about the project he was doing based on his trip to the sea life centre.

"Did you know," Billy said, for what felt like the thousandth time, "that the giant squid has eyes the size of Frisbees? There are three hundred types of squid, but there might be even more, because some live so deep in the ocean we haven't discovered them yet."

"Really?" Neena said. "That's amazing!"

And I could tell she meant it. Neena always meant everything she said. Not like most kids at school.

I could have joined in the conversation. I could have told them all about the firefly squid: how they only lived one year, and, at the end of their life, thousands of them gathered on a beach in Japan to lay eggs. How you could see their lights in the sea for miles, before they all faded away. But I didn't.

When we got home, I threw the door knocker back into Mum's trunk and locked it tight. It had caused enough trouble. Then I went to hide in Neena's room. I didn't come out again until dinnertime, where I hardly paused to look at what I was eating. Neena's parents had made lots of little different curries and chapatis and a big bowl of steaming rice. But I just shovelled it in. One spoonful after another, in an effort not to think about what had happened.

"I hear your mum's doing well," Mr Kapoor said. "That's good."

I nodded. But thinking about Mum and her black eye and bruised ribs made me feel worse. I stuffed some chapati into my mouth.

"Slow down," Billy signed.

"What was all that about animals coming into the school?" asked Mrs Kapoor.

I shrugged, stuffing a big spoonful of rice into my mouth so I didn't have to talk.

"A lot of weird things have been going on in this sleepy little town," said Mr Kapoor. "First earthquakes and then a stampede of animals in the school."

"Yeah, someone should really investigate what's going on, shouldn't they, Noah?" Neena said.

I could tell she was fed up of me ignoring her and was trying to get me to talk. But I just shrugged and ate another mouthful of curry.

Mrs Kapoor laid her hand on mine. "Leave him alone, Neena. He doesn't want to talk about any of this," she said.

"How do you know?" said Neena. "Maybe he does want to talk about it, Mum. Maybe everyone would feel better if they could just talk about things."

I had the feeling Neena wasn't talking about me any more. That she and her mum had fallen into an argument they were used to having.

"Neena, if Noah wants to talk about what's happened, he knows he can," Mrs Kapoor said firmly. "We're always here to listen, and so are his parents."

"Sure," Neena mumbled, and I saw her glance over at the photo of her sister. I hadn't noticed it before, but there were hardly any photos of her sister about. Just this one. "Except you don't, not really. You don't want to listen when I want to talk about Jasmin, do you?"

There was a silence.

"Who's for dessert?" Mr Kapoor said awkwardly.

"You're doing it again! Changing the subject." Neena put down her fork. "You won't even say her name. Well, I'll say it. Jasmin, Jasmin, Jasmin."

It felt like all the air had been sucked out the room. Mrs Kapoor swallowed and then stood and left the table. A moment later we heard the door shut and she appeared in the garden. Her back was to us, but I could see that her shoulders were hunched and stiff.

"I don't know what to say to you, Neena," Mr Kapoor said quietly. He stood and went out to join his wife.

I didn't know how to feel watching Neena's parents in the garden. They looked so small and sad out there. They had been so kind to me and Billy, but I knew how much Neena hurt. How much she missed her sister. I wondered for the first time if Neena also had a black bear in her stomach. If that's why she had got so upset when Jackson had snapped her butterfly bracelet. But it didn't excuse what she had done.

"What's going on?" Billy signed, looking completely confused.

"Family stuff," I signed back.

Billy nodded solemnly.

That night I lay in bed, gazing at the ceiling. The day's events kept playing over and over in a loop. At last I heard the door creak open and Neena whisper, "Noah? Are you awake?"

I pretended not to hear. I squeezed my eyes shut and pretended to snore.

"Noah, I know you don't snore," Neena sighed. "Come on. Now that we've found Helga, we have to plan what we're going to do next."

I pulled the duvet cover over my head. Billy moaned and then rolled over and went back to sleep.

"Look, I know you're mad," Neena whispered. "And I know I shouldn't have done what I did. Honestly, I'm not sure what came over me. But nobody got hurt, in the end. And it's not like you got into trouble."

"Trouble!" I said, throwing the cover off dramatically. "Of course I'm in trouble. I'm always in trouble. You just made everything worse!"

"How?" Neena asked.

"Now my friends know how weird I am. How can I ever go back?"

"You don't have to go back. We have the next clue. We can go find Helga now."

I shake my head. "I can't go right now, not after what happened. I have to go back and fix things first. Make everything right with Jackson, Dylan and Liam. If I break the curse, I want to be able to come back," I said.

"Why?" Neena asked, shaking her head like this was the maddest thing she had ever heard.

"Because I actually like it here, Neena! I *like* our school. I have friends. I fit in. I feel normal. Or at least I did. . ." I trailed off miserably.

"You know," Neena said, "if there was even a chance of fixing things for my family, there would be *nothing* that would stop me. And I wouldn't care what anyone thought."

"Well, that's because you're not normal!" I shouted.

The moment the words came out of my mouth I regretted them. I saw Neena's face crumple up.

"Neena, I didn't mean. . ." I started to apologize.

"Yes, you did," Neena snapped. "And you're right.

I'm not *normal* because I don't spend all my time worrying about fitting in. And that's *all* you worry about. So don't let me stop you from being normal and average and ordinary, because you're never going to be anything better." And she left the room, slamming the door shut behind her.

In the echoing emptiness of the room, Neena's words looped around and around in my head.

*Be normal, be average, be ordinary, because you're never going to be anything better.*

But Neena didn't know. She didn't know what it was like to never have a home, to be so different you had to learn how to hide it, to always be running. It was easy for her to say. Easy to think being normal was wrong. But actually, it's what everyone wants. Like llamas and goats, I knew that being in a pack is the only way to feel like you belong.

# CHAPTER 23

I knew as the first beams of light streamed through the window that the day was going to be horrible. After what Jackson, Dylan and Liam had seen, I was sure the school would be alight with hot little rumours that would be passed like lifelines through maths and science class. I was going to have to find a way to explain everything. Before everyone found out I was a freak.

One good thing was that Miss Ackerly had come back. She was sitting with the other teachers in assembly, happily chatting away. She didn't look sick; in fact she was looking surprisingly tanned. As we filed into the assembly hall, she looked up at me and winked.

Maybe with Miss Ackerly back, everything would

be OK after all. And we would finally be able to present our history project. That would give me a chance to smooth everything over with my friends.

I took my seat in assembly with the rest of my class, feeling a little lighter. Everyone was chatting away happily when Mr Hoad, our head teacher, walked up to the podium.

Everyone around me droned our customary, "Good morning, Mr Toad and Creatures."

Mr Hoad cleared his throat. He looked very cross. "Yesterday an incident rocked our school," he said dramatically. "We were invaded, no, *attacked* by our local wildlife," he carried on.

I stared straight ahead, unblinking. Trying desperately not to catch Jackson, Liam or Dylan's eye.

"And whilst we may not know what or who caused this incident—"

"It was Neena Kapoor and Noah Bradley," someone called out.

I wanted the floor to open up. And then I wanted to fall through it, down, down and straight to the hot centre of the earth. My cheeks were flaming red. And in front of me, I could see the back of Neena's neck, right under her ponytail, was flushed too.

Things got worse. In class, I saw that Liam, Dylan and Jackson had all moved from our normal table to a smaller one at the back. There wasn't any room for me. I tried to ignore the sinking feeling I felt. I went to sit in the empty seat next to Neena, but she gave me a furious glare and I backed away. I had to grab a chair and awkwardly bung it in at the end of a table of girls. They looked at me suspiciously, then went back to their conversation.

"OK then," Miss Ackerly said. "I hope you all missed me. It certainly seems like *I* missed quite a bit of excitement."

There was a low murmur of agreement.

"But since I'm back, how about we spend this lesson looking at those wonderful projects," Miss Ackerly continued.

The murmurs were replaced by a little ripple of excitement.

"Right then – could we have Jackson, Dylan, Liam and Noah to start things off," Miss Ackerly said. "Because this is very special indeed."

We all stood up. Jackson shot me a sly look. I knew that look. I'd seen it a hundred times. It was the look Jackson gave someone before he did something awful.

"We would be happy to present our project, miss," he said. "Only Noah's not part of our group. He works with Neena now. This is my, Liam's and Dylan's project, isn't it, boys?"

There was a short pause.

"Yeah, miss, that's right," Dylan said.

Liam was silent. Jackson elbowed him in the ribs. "Um, yeah," Liam mumbled.

"Is that true? I'm sure I had you marked down as a group," Miss Ackerly asked.

"Oh, we were, miss — but that was *before*..." Jackson said, letting the "before" hang in the air.

"Before what?" Miss Ackerly asked, looking increasingly confused.

Jackson shrugged. But I knew what he meant. *Before* I had started hanging out with Neena. *Before* I had released a horde of animals on him. *Before* he knew who I really was.

"Right," said Miss Ackerly slowly. Her eyes went from one to another of us and I could tell she was trying to work out what was going on. "So, you didn't work on this project, Noah?"

I looked over at Liam. I knew if I could only catch his eye, he would tell the truth. But Liam didn't look up. He just shifted awkwardly. It was three against one.

"No," I said at last.

"Right. So, do you and Neena have a project, Noah? I don't think I see one on my desk."

"It's at home, miss," Neena jumped in.

"OK," Miss Ackerly said. "How about we look at half the projects today and the other half in the next lesson. Then we can award the trophy."

I looked at the big silver cup on Miss Ackerly's desk. It had the names of everyone who had ever won it engraved on the front. I had spent so long imagining my name added to the top.

I watched as Jackson, Dylan and Liam presented the project without me. Jackson even did a big theatrical bow when the whole class clapped at the end. My whole body filled with anger. I imagined myself getting bigger and bigger, like a puffer fish. I wanted so badly to say something before I exploded. But I knew I couldn't. I couldn't stand up to Jackson. Not if I ever wanted things to go back to the way they were.

# CHAPTER 24

I was sure the day couldn't get any worse. But as soon as we pulled up to number 17 Verity Close, I realized I was wrong.

The front door was open, the window was smashed, and the curtains billowed out into the street.

"Stay here," Mr Kapoor said, getting out of the car. "Don't come in till I tell you it's OK."

I watched him go into the house. Forever seemed to pass before he appeared at the doorway and beckoned us in.

"What happened?" asked Mrs Kapoor, hurrying after him. We followed and stopped dead inside.

The whole place had been ransacked. There was glass everywhere. Through the hallway, into the living room. A mirror was smashed. Drawers were pulled out. The neat house had been turned upside down.

Inside the kitchen it was even worse. All the drawers, even the fridge, had been emptied out.

"I can't understand it," Mr Kapoor said, shaking his head. A carton of milk spurted out on to the floor. "Nothing seems to have been taken."

Billy yelped "Arnold!" and ran off to the shed. Neena caught my eye.

"The trunk," she whispered.

And all the fighting and arguing we had done earlier dropped away. We both bolted upstairs.

Jasmin's room was just as bad as downstairs. All the wardrobe drawers were pulled out. The globe was lying on the floor; the travel books had been thrown about, their pages crumpled and torn. One of the cupboard doors hung limply. I flung the other door back and saw the trunk had been pulled out from its hiding place. We both leaned in and pulled it out. In the light of the room we could see the lock was broken. I threw the lid back and groaned.

The diary, the letters, the door knocker and even the photo of Helga; all of it was gone.

"Oh no!" I groaned, sliding down the side of the wardrobe and collapsing on to the floor. "Mr Grey has the door knocker. That means he has all of its magic and power – and we'll never stand a chance of reuniting the objects."

"Unless it wasn't in the trunk after all," said Billy, slipping into the room with Arnold around his neck. He sheepishly pulled the fox face door knocker from his bag.

"Billy!" I gasped. "I told you to leave it here!"

"I know. But everyone in my class was talking about the magic door knocker that day. I may have taken it in and shown it to some friends. I didn't use it or anything. I didn't even tell them it was magic. . ." Billy trailed off.

"I should be mad, but I honestly couldn't love you any more right now," I said as I wrapped Billy up in a bone-crunching brother hug and Neena laughed and joined in.

"Ow, you're suffocating me," Billy said, but he hugged us back.

I put the knocker into my rucksack.

"That's a relief," I said. "Finally, some good news."

I looked up, to see that Billy and Neena had fallen quiet.

Neena was staring at Jasmin's room, finally taking in all the mess. I looked too, seeing it for the first time. Amid all the chaos I could see the picture of

Neena and her sister had been smashed, probably as the drawers had been thrown open, and the hanging glass butterflies had fallen to the floor. Some were broken and cracked. Little rainbow pieces of glass glinted up from the carpet.

"Oh, Neena," I said, and I went over to her.

She backed away.

"I'm fine," she said flatly, but I knew she wasn't.

"I'm sorry," I said. "I'm really, really sorry."

"You can stop saying that," Neena said, turning away.

But I was sorry. Sorry I'd been cruel to her at school. Sorry I'd called her a freak. But most of all, sorry I had brought all this trouble to her and her family.

The police had arrived by the time Billy and I went downstairs.

"So, is there anything missing – jewellery, electronics, valuables?" the officer was saying.

"That's the odd thing," Mrs Kapoor said. "Nothing seems to be missing."

The officer made a scratchy note on her notepad.

"How odd. You've no idea what they could have been after?" she asked. "Because it looks like they were going to stop at nothing to find it."

Billy and I looked at each other. We knew it would

only be a matter of time before Mr Grey came back. The door knocker wasn't safe here any more and neither were we.

It was time to go find Helga.

# CHAPTER 25

It was four a.m. when my alarm went off. I didn't need it; I'd been lying awake for hours, thoughts racing around in my head.

*Could I really leave?*

*Would we be safe?*

*Would Helga Ogberry really be able to help us?*

I was already dressed. I went to wake Billy, then stopped. I needed to leave a note for Neena. I ripped out a page from one of my school workbooks and began writing.

*Dear Neena,*

*When you read this, Billy and I will be gone.*
*You know where. Don't be mad we left without*

*you. I didn't want to get you into any more trouble.*
*Because you are my friend. Even if I haven't been*
*very good at showing it.*

  *Goodbye,*
  *Noah*


I woke Billy and Arnold and slipped the note under Jasmin's bedroom door. Then we crept down the stairs.

"Are you sure we should do this?" Billy asked.

His lip was wobbling. He looked so little in the dark kitchen dressed in one of my big oversized T-shirts and stroking Arnold. I bent down so that I could look in his face.

"You want to break the curse, don't you?"

Billy nodded his head.

"Well, then we need Helga; she'll help us," I said.

"But Mum said it was too dangerous," Billy said in his smallest voice.

I knelt and put my arms gently on his shoulders.

"Mr Grey is after the door knocker. It's not safe here any more and neither are we."

"But what if it's not safe at this Miss Helga's place either?"

I sighed. "I guess we just have to find out."

Billy shivered. "I'm scared, Noah," he signed.

"Me too," I signed back. "But you know what we do when were scared?" I said.

"Close our eyes and think of one good thing," Billy said, closing his eyes. "I'm thinking of the massive ferret run Dad could build for Arnold if we didn't have to move all the time."

"That's a good one," I said.

"And if we broke the curse and I wasn't scared all the time then maybe I wouldn't have to get into bed with you," Billy added. "I could sleep in my own bed, maybe even without having my Batman night light on."

"Yeah," I said, feeling like something was caught in my throat. "That would be good too. So, are you up for this?"

"So long as we can bring food," Billy said, leading me into the kitchen.

I opened my bag and started filling it with bags of crisps from the kitchen cupboard. I was just about to zip up my bag when a light flicked on. I spun around.

"You don't really think you're going without me, do you?" Neena whispered fiercely.

"Didn't you read my letter?" I hissed.

"Yes. You said you were my friend. And I'm not letting my friends go on a dangerous mission alone," Neena said, a small smile flickering across her face. "And you two won't survive two minutes out there.

Not when the only things you've packed are crisps and an incontinent ferret."

"We packed other stuff," I said. "And Arnold's housetrained."

"Mostly," Billy added.

Neena shook her head. "If you're going to run away, you need to have a plan. To be organized."

Neena thumped a large duffel bag on the kitchen table that I recognized as her running away bag. She unzipped it with a flourish.

Neena had thought of everything. There was a sleeping bag. Snacks. A map. Clothes. And a wallet full of money.

"I can't let you come with us," I said, trying to sound firm.

"Why?" Neena hissed.

I knew how hard things were for Neena, but I also knew all the reasons she should stay. Her parents loved her, even if they didn't always know how to show it. Her house was safe and warm. She never had to worry about the ceiling falling in or having to live in a van. She didn't have to lie to social workers or make up stories about her past. And most importantly, if she left, people would miss her.

"Because you're not cursed," I said. "You can stay here. For ever if you want."

Neena snorted. "Why would I want to do that? You've seen what's it like for me here. School is the worst. And at home no one talks about anything real, ever."

I could see her mind was made up.

"It's dangerous," I said.

"It wouldn't be an adventure if it wasn't dangerous," Neena said.

Billy watched both of us and stroked Arnold thoughtfully.

"What do you think?" I said, turning to him.

Billy sighed dramatically. "I don't want you two arguing all the time," he said.

"We won't," Neena said, flashing me a look. "Plus, I packed snacks," she said, pulling out a tube of Smarties and a family pack of cheesy nachos from the lid of the rucksack.

"In that case, welcome aboard," Billy said, holding out his hand.

Neena laughed and shook it.

All three of us crept back down the hallway.

"OK then," I said, adjusting the strap on my backpack and reaching for the doorknob. "Ready?"

Everyone nodded, suddenly serious again.

The door creaked open. Moonlight flooded the hallway. I took a deep breath and then stepped out into the night, followed by the shadow of my brother and best friend.

No one glanced out their window, or switched on their light, to see three children and a ferret heading off into the night. A cat crossed our path, an owl hooted, and before we knew it, we were at the end of the cul-de-sac.

I looked back at Verity Close one last time, before we turned on to the main road. I wasn't sure if we were ever coming back. The world under the light of the stars suddenly felt very big.

# CHAPTER 26

It took us nearly an hour of walking to the train station. Neena had worked out the whole plan the day we had discovered Helga's address in the library. She had researched the trains and planned the route, even borrowed her mum's credit card to help buy us the tickets. I was suddenly very glad she had insisted on coming.

"We need to get the first train to London and then get a coach from London to Port Mullen," Neena said as we arrived in the ticket hall.

"That's a lot of trains," I said. "We just have to make our connection in London," Neena said, scanning the arrivals board.

"And if we miss it?" I asked.

"I have a backup plan," Neena said.

I looked at the station, deserted apart from a man in a ticket booth. If we turned back now, I thought, we could be back in bed before Mr and Mrs Kapoor woke up. I could pretend this curse was all just a horrible nightmare. Something that was happening to someone else.

"We can't go back, not now," Neena said, as if reading my mind.

I looked at Billy. His face was filled with expectation. He needed me to be brave. He needed me to be his big brother. I had failed him once, when I failed to protect him from the earthquake. I wouldn't do it again.

I nodded, once.

"OK then. Let's do this," Neena said, striding up to the ticket counter.

The small ticket booth was filled up with a large man reading the paper. He didn't look up as we walked over, just coughed and turned the pages of his paper.

"I'm collecting three tickets to London King's Cross, please," Neena said, showing the man a reference number. The ticket attendant eyed us suspiciously. I adjusted my backpack and tried to look bored. As if it was perfectly normal for three kids to be getting a train to London on their own first thing in the morning.

"It's just the three of you, then?" the ticket attendant asked, as Arnold's head popped out of Billy's jumper. Billy quickly pushed him back down.

"Yes, just us," Neena said firmly.

"It's a long way to London." The man pointed at Billy. "He looks awfully young."

"I'm eight and a quarter," Billy said.

"And we're very responsible," I added.

"Hmm," the ticket inspector said, "all the same, I think I should ring one of your parents."

I felt a flood of panic. We had been caught before we'd even stepped on to the train.

"You can't," Neena said, jumping in. "Mum's in hospital and we've been sent to stay with our grandparents until she gets better. They don't drive any more, which is why we're getting the train. Granddad's meeting us off it. Platform five at nine a.m. If you want, you could try ringing him. His number's 07700900927. But he's not very good with phones, gets a bit confused with the buttons." Neena paused for breath.

The ticket inspector considered us all again for a second.

"If you want to ring, can you do it now? Because our train's due in a few minutes. And I don't want to miss it because the next one's not for hours," Neena said. "And our grandad—"

"All right, all right," the inspector sighed, holding his hands up. "Your train's on platform two. Here's your tickets."

As the train pulled up to the station, a little part of me hoped to see Mr and Mrs Kapoor running to stop us. But I knew the only person who was coming after us was Mr Grey. We climbed on to the train. I glanced behind me nervously as we waited for the doors to close. The station was deserted. Would Mr Grey pursue us all the way to Port Mullen? I wondered. I felt the door knocker sitting heavy in the bottom of my bag. How could something so small and so old cause so much trouble? The train doors beeped, the railway attendant whistled, and the train jerked away from the platform.

We all sat quietly. There was no one else in the carriage – it was too early. As the train picked up speed, I thought of Mum lying in hospital and Dad flying to meet us, and Mr and Mrs Kapoor about to wake up to empty beds. I hoped what I was doing was right. I hoped I could keep us safe. Billy squeezed my hand and we watched as the town blended into greys and greens before slipping out of sight.

# CHAPTER 27

I must have fallen asleep, because before I knew it Neena was shaking me awake.

"Noah, we're nearly there. Our station is the next stop."

I rubbed my bleary eyes. Hazy sunlight streamed into the carriage and I could see the silhouettes of skyscrapers and office buildings rush past us. Neena was biting her lip and looking out of the window.

"What's wrong?" I asked.

"Nothing," she said. "It's just ... Mum and Dad will be up by now. They'll have noticed I'm gone."

"But you said back in the house you wanted to get away from them," I said, puzzled.

"I said that so I could come with you."

"And you tried to run away before," I said, thinking of the night I'd stopped Neena sneaking out. The night the birds had come.

"I wasn't running away, Noah," Neena said scornfully.

"Well, what were you doing that night?"

She stared at her shoes for a moment. Then she took a deep breath.

"It was my sister's birthday. And it had come and gone without anyone mentioning her. Not once. I felt like she was ... disappearing all over again. Like we were forgetting her. So, I planned to do something special."

"What?" I asked.

Neena lifted her chin. "I was going to spread her ashes. I wanted her to be somewhere nice. Not cooped up in some jar."

I thought about when Nan died. We had spread her ashes across the sea where she had been living, in Cornwall. Mum had said it was so she could always be on a journey.

And even though I had been a bit sad about it – I had wanted a place to go and visit, like a gravestone - now every time I looked at the ocean it reminded me of her. I liked to think of her visiting the coral reefs or forgotten shipwrecks.

"I wish I could help," I said at last.

Neena smiled at me. "I'd like that. But let me help you first, Noah. I'll get you to Helga so you can break your curse."

Neena made it all sound so easy. I thought about that boy, who had cycled through Verity Close with his mates, who had no idea his home would be destroyed for ever. I wanted him back. But I couldn't help thinking about Mum's warning.

And then I realized something. Mr Grey had Mum's notebook, with all of its names and, circled in red, Helga Bradley. He had the photo and her letter. There was no address, though. It would be hard to figure out where she lived from the photo and a name.

But we had, I thought. And with an icy shiver I realized Mr Grey could too.

# CHAPTER 28

We got off the train at Kings Cross station and stepped into the early morning crush of people.

"We need to get to a coach station," Neena said, checking her watch. "The next one to Port Mullen is in half an hour. They don't run that often, so we better be quick."

"How do we get there?" I asked.

"We get the Tube," Neena said. "It shouldn't be too far. I hope."

But London was much bigger and more confusing than I had expected. There were so many different coloured lines on the Tube map, and everything was so fast and busy, that we all got confused. And we didn't want to ask anyone for directions in case they started asking questions. So it took us three attempts to find our right train. By the time we arrived at Victoria we had to run to the coach station.

But just as we turned the corner into the big stone archway, Billy stopped dead.

"What's wrong?" I asked.

"Look," Billy signed, pointing across the forecourt towards our coach.

Neena peered around the corner and then ducked back, turning pale.

"Oh, Noah," she said.

My stomach lurched.

"What is it?" I didn't really want to know the answer.

"Just look," Neena said.

All three of us craned our necks around the stone gateway. There was a thick crowd waiting around two coaches being loaded up. But in between them and us, through the smoke, I could see the tall, thin silhouette of Mr Grey.

We all ducked back behind the pillar.

"Why is he here?" Billy said.

"For the same reason we are," Neena groaned. "To find Helga and the rest of the gifts. He must have figured out where she lives."

I peered around the corner again.

Mr Grey was lining up for the coach. He was carrying his big battered briefcase.

The coach to Port Mullen had just pulled to our bay. It hissed to a stop, the door opened, and a stream of people began getting off. The coach driver, a man in a red cap, got off to help unload everyone's bags from the hold underneath.

"We have to find a way to stop him getting on that coach," Neena said.

"Could we get the police?" Billy said.

"What would we tell them? I don't think they'd believe the truth. Besides, as three runaways, we really need to avoid them," Neena said.

"We could use the door knocker," I said, knowing even as I said it that it was a terrible idea.

Neena shook her head. "No," she said firmly. "It's too risky. Mr Grey would know for sure we were here then. Plus, there's too many people; they could get hurt."

"But we have to do something," I said, just as a recorded message burbled over the tannoy in the coach station.

*"If you see something that doesn't look right, speak to a member of staff or police. See it, say it, sorted."*

We all leaned around the wall and watched Mr Grey. He was fussing with his bag. The coach driver was insisting he had to put it in with the baggage.

"It's too large to take on board," we could hear the driver yell.

But Mr Grey shook his head, clasping the suitcase to his chest. He wouldn't hand it over no matter how much the driver seemed to be insisting.

"That looks awfully suspicious, doesn't it?" I said.

Neena grinned, cottoning on to my idea. "Certainly does," she said. "Think we should go tell someone?"

There was a transport police officer standing by the station. I went over. "Excuse me," I said nervously. "But there's a man over there acting very suspiciously."

The women wrinkled her forehead in concern. "Could you explain what you saw?" she said.

"He keeps reaching for something in his bag," I said.

The women nodded. "Do you think you could point him out to me?" she asked.

I picked out Mr Grey in the crowd. He still had his hand in his bag as if he couldn't let go of something very precious, and close up we could see how sweaty and nervous he looked. The woman hesitated, then picked up a walkie-talkie on her belt. "Best to be safe," she said, and spoke into it. "OK, I'm sending someone to check out what you've reported."

I rejoined Neena and Billy, careful to keep out of

sight of Mr Grey. It wasn't long before we saw two police officers making their way purposefully through the crowd.

Mr Grey was scanning the area, his eyes pale and cold. He saw the police officers just before they approached, and his expression flickered. Then he turned and ran, clutching his bag. The two police officers immediately gave chase. There's was a huge, worried gasp from the crowd, and me and Neena looked at each other.

"I didn't think he would run," Neena said. "I wonder why he did that?"

"I don't know," I replied. "Helga said he was dangerous, so who knows what he might be wanted for?"

"Or maybe he really is hiding something in that bag," Billy added ominously.

We could hear police radios crackle and see blue lights in the distance. The whole terminal was abuzz with what happened. Then a few moments later a women's voice came over the tannoy.

"All coaches are to continue boarding."

"All right," the coach driver said, stepping out and holding his arms up, "show's over. Let's keep to schedule."

The murmurs in the crowd died down and

everyone started boarding again. Me, Neena and Billy slipped into our line. It wasn't long until we were at the front. Neena flashed our tickets. The coach driver looked behind us.

"Where's your parents?" he asked.

"Mum's just at the back, I had to take my brother to the loo," Neena said confidently.

"Mum, save us a seat," I yelled, waving to a confused-looking woman at the back.

The driver sighed and waved us on. Me, Neena and Billy rushed to the row of seats at the back. We fell into them, giggling.

As the coach pulled out, we passed the police bundling Mr Grey into the back of a squad car. I tried to duck out of sight, but he saw me, and I saw his face twist into a furious grimace. The same look I'd seen at the hospital when the lights had gone out and again when he'd tried to throw me down the stairs.

"He's seen us," Neena breathed.

"We may have slowed him down. But he's not going to stop, is he? And it looks like he knows where we're going."

I shook my head and looked down at Billy, who was curled up on my lap and already snoring peacefully. A terrible feeling stirred in the pit of my stomach.

"What are we going to do?" Neena asked,

nervously twisting the end of her plait.

It was the first time I had ever seen her looking frightened. If *she* was afraid, then we were really in trouble. But there was no turning back now.

"We're just going to have to beat him to Helga," I said, setting my jaw firmly.

# CHAPTER 29

By the time the coach arrived in Port Mullen it was sunny and warm. The smell of vinegary fish and chips wafted on the breeze. Seagulls whirled around in the air, looking for chips to steal, and the gentle slap of the waves washed over the excited screams of holidaymakers on the beach. But we couldn't join in with the excitement of everyone leaving the coach. They were all there for holidays and ice cream. None of them had to worry about breaking a curse.

"I'm tired," Billy said, pulling at my sleeve.

"Me too, bud, but we have to keep moving," I said.

"And I'm hungry," he said.

We hadn't eaten anything but a handful of pickled

onion crisps and half-stale biscuits on the coach, and
I could feel my belly rumbling.

"Me too," Neena said. "Let's get an ice cream. We
need to ask for directions anyway."

"OK then," I said.

We walked down the hilly slope past the colourful
fisherman houses and towards the bay. Sunlight
bounced off the flat clear water as our trainers sank
into the wet sand and slipped over the wet pebbles. We
stopped at a faded yellow ice cream van and Neena
pulled out the last of her emergency money to order us
three Mr Whippy ice creams with rainbow sprinkles.

"We're looking for someone; you wouldn't be
able to help us, would you?" Neena asked the woman
serving us.

She leaned out. Her face was cheerful and tanned.

"All's roight, I'm Pat," she said, offering us a big
warm hand. "I knows just about everyone around
here," she continued in a thick sing-songy accent.
"Who's it you little ones be looking for?"

"Helga Ogberry?" I said.

"Oh, we all know Helga, lives just up the hill, in
the old cottage at the very end of Cliff Lane, big creepy
old place, you can't miss it," she said, pointing off to
the distance. She gave us a curious look. "Strange lady
though, that Helga. Not a big fan of visitors."

I could feel the black bear stirring in my stomach. What if Helga wouldn't let us in? I licked my ice cream for something to do. I watched a boy smack a huge beach ball at his dad and a little girl riding on her mum's shoulders, laughing away in the sea. I felt an ache watching them. I would have given anything to be part of a normal family, having a normal day at the beach.

"So, she doesn't have many people round then?" Neena asked.

The woman shook her head. "No, old Helga, she's always been a loner." She leaned out further. "Arrived nearly a year ago, in the middle of the night, on a rowboat of all things. With just the one suitcase. Most days she's out all hours walking the cliffs, watching the skies. What she's looking for, no one's quite sure."

But I knew. She was looking for the black birds from the north.

"But you're visiting her?" Pat said curiously.

"We're family," Billy said. "She's expecting us."

"Oh," Pat said, looking flustered. "Lovely. I beg your pardon. I'm sure she's a roight charming lady once you get to know her. Come for your summer holiday, have you?"

I nodded.

"Well, enjoy yourself and tell Helga I say hello," Pat said, adding an extra sprinkle of hundreds and thousands to Billy's cone with a wink.

We ate our ice creams walking up the steep, winding cobbled lanes in the direction the woman had pointed us in. We passed old-fashioned shops selling hand-made kites and bright toys and dingy-looking pubs with names like the Black Bear, the Fat Friar and the Crow's Nest Inn painted on their wooden signs. Until, finally, we got to the bottom of Cliff Lane. It was a steep, never-ending road up. Squinting, I could just make out a church spire way off at the top.

"Why does everything always have to be up a hill?" I groaned.

But Neena looked at me with the biggest, widest grin. A smile that lit up her whole face. I'd almost forgotten what Neena looked like without a scowl, so all I could do was blink.

"Look, Noah, look!" Neena said, pointing to a tumbledown cottage at the very top of the lane.

In the window was a lantern.

*A lantern that once lit could control the tides, protecting them from the temperamental sea.*

"It couldn't be the one from the legend, could it?" Billy said.

"I think it just might be," I said.

I felt something stir in me that I hadn't felt in a very long time.

Hope.

# CHAPTER 30

The hummingbird can flap its wings seventy times a second, and its heart beats over a thousand beats a minute. Standing at the gate to Helga's cottage, I was pretty sure I knew what the hummingbird felt like.

"Are you sure this is the place?" I asked nervously.

The cottage loomed over us, but it was nothing like I had imagined from the newspaper article, or even Pat the ice cream lady's description. I was expecting a haunted crumbling ruin, but whilst the cottage was very old and ramshackle, it still looked like something from a seaside postcard. It had a sagging thatched roof, white walls covered in twisted vines, and around the low stone wall grew thick, tangled rose bushes.

"This is it," Neena said as she pushed open the rusty gate.

Under the high arch of the doorway I took a deep breath before knocking loudly at the door. For a moment there was nothing but silence within. We stood on the slope of the cliffs, listening to the rustle of trees in the wind, the squawk of the seagulls circling above and the eerie squeak of the gate rocking back and forth. Then there was the faintest sound within. And then the light slap of feet against a hard floor, before the door was cautiously opened. Helga Ogberry stood barefoot, frowning at us. She had a wrinkly long neck, hunched shoulders and was wearing an ugly high-necked jumper. She looked nothing like the glamourous women in Mum's picture, dancing and laughing away. She looked more like a very old turtle. But even in the dim light of entranceway I could see Helga's brilliant green Bradley eyes. She stared at me curiously.

"Yes?" she said.

"I think you can help—" was all I could manage to get out before Helga snapped, "Not interested," and slammed the door shut.

We all looked at each other, stunned.

"She seems nice," Billy said.

I knocked again. This time it opened more quickly, as though Helga was waiting by the door. She opened it a crack and peered round suspiciously.

"I've been looking for you for a long time," I said quickly, ready to pour out our whole story. "My name is Noah—"

"I'm still not interested," Helga said, slamming the door shut again.

"Maybe we should come back later?" Billy said.

"We can't," I said desperately. "She's in danger from Mr Grey, she just doesn't know it yet."

I took another deep breath and then hammered at the door, not stopping until Helga flung it open.

"No. I do not want to subscribe to a paper, receive elderly care, have my windows cleaned or become a Jehovah's Witness. So please, go away," she said.

"I can't," I said, and from my bag I pulled out the fox door knocker.

Helga's eyes grew wide and her mouth puckered into a little round O.

"Is that. . ." She swallowed. "Is that what I think it is?"

"I think you're Helga Bradley," I said. "And I think you know how to break the curse."

She stared at me for a long moment. "Well, what are you waiting out there for? Come in, come in," she said, beckoning us into the dimly lit cottage.

Inside, the cottage was very bare. There was a

battered armchair in front of a little portable TV, stacks of books, and an open suitcase by the front door. There was a basket of wood before a wood-burning fire, a handful of photographs from different places in the world, an oriental-looking lamp and a Mexican tiled mirror hanging on the wall. Helga had been here a year, but she was still camping out, I thought. Not bothering to unpack. Just like we had for so many years.

"Excuse the mess," Helga said, picking her way over to the chair. She pulled out some half-packed boxes for us to sit on. "You've caught me at a bad time. I think it's moving time again."

We all jumped as the mirror slipped off the wall and cracked into sharp pieces that shimmered up from the floor.

"Sorry," Helga said, sighing. "Things like that have been happening all week."

"The bad omens?" Billy asked.

Helga nodded. "I reckon I only have a day or two left before the birds show up. Which is why I'm very glad you're here," she said. She frowned. "But where's your mother?"

I started to explain everything that had happened. About how our house had been destroyed in an earthquake. How Mum had been injured and Mr

Grey had shown up at the hospital to try and find out where the door knocker was and had been pursuing us ever since.

"He pretended to be an insurance person," I said. "But we knew that something wasn't right."

"He didn't say anything about me?" Helga asked anxiously.

"No," I said.

Helga's grip on the armchair relaxed. "Go on," she said.

"Anyway, Mum gave us the key to the trunk, and we managed to get to it before Mr Grey did. And that's when we found your letter. And how you told Mum you thought breaking the curse meant we had to unite the objects."

"How did you find me?" Helga asked. "I thought I'd done a good job of hiding. I changed my name, I move every year..."

"Mum had a photo," I said. "You're at a wedding, wearing a shimmery green dress. We managed to track you down from that."

Helga's expression became distant.

"Oh yes," she said softly. "I bought that dress for the wedding. I got it in Paris; it was made of the softest silk and had the most delicate beadwork." Her thin, delicate fingers traced it in the air. "I used to love wearing it to parties with friends." Her expression cleared and she shook her head. "But it's been a while since I've been to a party, even longer since I had friends. It was wiser to push them away, keep them safe. Keep myself safer. The way we Bradleys have to live. . ." She shrugged. "Not everyone understands."

I thought about Mum and Dad, and him saying he was tired of moving all the time and going off to Singapore. But he was coming back, I thought. I hoped.

"The thing is," Neena said, "Mr Grey broke in and found the photo and figured out where you live too. We got here before him, but I don't think he'll be far behind."

"And he will stop at nothing to get the door knocker. So, we need to unite all the objects to break the curse before he gets here," I finished.

"Ah," Helga said. "That's not as easy as it sounds."

"What?" I said, confused. "Why not?"

"Well," said Helga, smiling, "I have the lantern." She walked to the window and lifted it.

Billy smiled. *"The lantern that could control the tempestuous tides,"* he quoted softly.

Helga nodded and reached into her pocket and pulled out a set of matches. With a quick stroke she lit it. It filled the room with a soft glow. She put the lantern back in the window and we could see the tide edge away from the shore.

"And," she said, walking to the fireplace, "I have the fire poker."

She strode over to the fireplace and lifted a battered iron poker from the wood basket. With a flick of her wrist the fire poker shot out a small blue flame that slowly crackled into a roaring blue fire.

"*The fire poker with the never-ending flames, to hold the ice and the snow at bay,*" I said, joining Helga to warm my hands over them.

"And you have the door knocker," Helga said.

I lifted it out of my pocket. It felt buzzy in my hand again.

"*The door knocker that could summon the animals of the earth for protection from the wolves,*" I said.

I went to snap it shut, but Helga held up her hand.

"Perhaps we don't need a demonstration of *that*," Helga said.

"So, there's just one more," Billy said. "*The weathervane that could channel the wind and lighting to protect against the mischievous stars.*"

"And that, my dear children, is where we run into problems," Helga said. "Because as you can see, I don't have it."

"But your letter said you had the other three gifts,"

Neena said, open-mouthed.

"I said I knew where they were. Not that I had them," Helga said.

"Then who does have it?" I said.

"I think you know," Helga said.

And suddenly everything fell into place. Why Mr Grey had carried his bag everywhere. Why he had been checking it so anxiously in the train station. And how when he had reached into it at the hospital, all the lights had blinked and flickered.

Mr Grey had the weathervane.

# CHAPTER 31

"How did he get hold of it?" I asked.

"We Bradleys, we've tried to keep our gifts safe, hidden. But powerful things can't stay secret for ever," said Helga. "Somehow Mr Grey must have found out about them and he's been hunting for them ever since. But not to break the curse. He wants to be the owner of their power."

"But we need all four gifts to break the curse, don't we?" Billy said quietly.

We had come all this way, risking everything, and for nothing. I felt like the floor was opening and I could feel myself tumbling, tumbling into it. Billy stood frozen, his lip wobbling. Helga stood by the fire looking grey and motheaten. I could feel a tornado building inside me, of all the feeling and emotions I didn't want to share. I was shaking trying to keep them all in. I couldn't be brave Noah any more. Or cool Noah. Or even big brother Noah. Our adventure had come to an end. And I had failed. Tears prickled in the corners of my eyes. I looked up at the paper lampshade on the ceiling, throwing out light in a big star shape. I thought of our family endlessly following the North Star, forever trying to find a home we would never be able to keep. I could no longer hold back the tears. They erupted in deep, snotty, body-shaking sobs. Both Billy and Neena threw their arms around me. Even Helga awkwardly patted my back. But in all the dramatics, we had forgotten Arnold was still in Billy's backpack – until he popped his head out of the bag, sniffing the air and chattering madly.

Helga froze, then hopped up on to the armchair with surprising speed. She removed one shoe and held it aloft.

"Why," she said, "is there a rat in your backpack?"

Billy drew himself up. "How could you? Arnold is *not* a rat," he said firmly. "Tell him, Noah."

My tears had turned to laughter. Helga's suspicious face and Billy's outraged one were too funny, and in the meantime, Arnold had wriggled away and was now sticking his head into a brass pot.

"He's a ferret," I explained. Helga didn't look any less concerned.

"A pet ferret," I added.

Helga seemed to relax. Neena grabbed the other shoe from Helga's hand. And I helped her gently down from the chair.

"How could you think Arnold was a rat? Ferrets are nothing like them. They are much smarter, for one thing," Billy said.

Helga raised an eyebrow. Arnold had got stuck in the pot he had upturned, and his back end was wriggling madly trying to free himself. Billy bent down to pull him out.

"He's not at his best. He's had a long journey and he's tired and hungry and fed up," Billy said, cradling Arnold against his chest.

I knew just how Arnold felt. I hadn't eaten any food since the ice cream and that felt like a very long time ago. Helga looked down at the small gold watch on her wrist and then she glanced out of the window. I hadn't realized how much time had passed. It was already getting dark.

"I think we could all do with some food," she said.

"But what if Mr Grey arrives?" Neena asked.

"Coaches will have stopped running by now. The earliest he can get here is tomorrow," Helga said.

"Well, you can bet he'll be on the earliest coach down," Neena said darkly.

"Exactly," Helga said. Her expression was thoughtful. "Which means we know when and where he'll be arriving."

"And how does that help us?" Neena asked.

"It gives us the advantage," Helga said. "That is, if you're not too afraid to take it?"

There was a silence.

"He has what is ours," Helga said fiercely. "Without that weathervane, the curse will never be broken. And I don't know about you, but I'd like to stay in one place for longer than a year."

We all looked at each other and nodded. I saw the flicker of a smile pass across Helga's face.

"Good," she said, clapping her hands decisively. "It's decided then. We will find a way to get back what Mr Grey stole. But first, food," she added.

Helga made us a strange but delicious feast of everything that was left in her cupboards. Soggy ginger cake, tomato soup, boiled lentils, mystery meat from a tin that had lost its label, sardines and stale crackers. But I was so hungry I ate the lot.

And all the while, my brain had been working

away. As we sat in front of the fire with slabs of chocolate, I said, "I think I have an idea on how we're going to get the weathervane."

Helga, who was clasping an enormous mug of tea, smiled. "I thought you had been quiet. So, how are we going to do it?"

"By taking it from right under his nose," I replied.

Nobody said a word. I watched Neena's and Billy's frightened faces lit up by the roaring blue fire. I could see their trepidation. After all, how could three kids, an old woman and a ferret stop Mr Grey? Finally, Billy said what everyone was thinking.

"But how? He always has it with him in his bag."

"Exactly. His bag. But there's one time when he won't be holding it," I said.

"On the coach. They make you put all the bags in the hold!" Neena gasped.

I pointed a finger at her.

"Got it," I said. "And we know he'll be on the first coach. So why don't we go down to meet him?"

"A nice welcome committee," Helga said, her eyes sparkling.

"But he'll see us!" Billy said, squeezing poor Arnold so tight he squealed in protest and nipped at his finger.

"Maybe not. Maybe if we cause a distraction big

enough, one of us can slip into the crowd and steal his briefcase from the coach hold," I said.

"What sort of distraction will be big enough that Mr Grey won't notice us sneaking into the coach hold under his nose?" Neena asked.

"I don't know," I say, rubbing my forehead. "It has to be something flashy, something he can't miss. . ."

Both Billy and Neena rolled their eyes. But a wicked grin flashed across Helga's face.

"I have an idea," she said

"What?" we all said together.

"We use this," Helga said, lifting the lantern from the window.

# CHAPTER 32

By the time we went to bed, it was very late. We snuggled up under Neena's green sleeping bag, on the creaky camp bed Helga had set up for us in the living room. I fell asleep right away, exhausted by our day.

That night I dreamed about Verity Close for the first time since the earthquake. Dad was fixing it up with magic bricks and Mum was decorating my room again. Only this time she was making it a real jungle and filling it full of all kinds of animals, like parrots and monkeys and even a lion. And then Jackson and Dylan and Liam all came around and were dead impressed by my bedroom jungle. Even Jackson, who had pulled a shiny silver cup from his bag and offered to it me.

"I want to share the history cup with you, Noah," Jackson said. "We couldn't have won it without you."

I was just reaching for it when Neena shook me awake.

"What, what?" I said groggily.

"I need to talk to you," Neena hissed.

I rolled over in my sleeping bag and pulled myself up into a sitting position on the end of the camp bed. Rubbing my eyes, I asked, "What about?"

"It's the plan. Something feels wrong to me."

I yawned. "Which bit?"

Neena walked to the window, looking out and rubbing her arms for warmth.

"Well, for one thing, I don't think Helga's thought it all through. I'm worried she wants the weathervane back, no matter what the risks. It's . . . desperate."

"Of course she does," I said. "She's desperate to break the curse. You try leaving everything and everyone behind again and again, and you'd see how *desperate* you feel."

"I've got other questions too," Neena said.

I sighed. "Like what?" I asked.

"Like, why didn't she tell your mum everything about Mr Grey in her letter?"

"I don't know, maybe she wanted to explain

everything in person or maybe she didn't want to scare her," I replied wearily.

"Yeah, I guess," Neena said.

But she stayed standing over by the window, shivering. The moonlight cut across her face and I could see the worry in her brown eyes.

"We have to get the weathervane off Mr Grey," I said. "Or else we'll all be running for ever. We'll never have a real home, and neither will Helga, and that's no way to live. Mum started this and we have to finish it."

"She also warned us. She warned us that he was dangerous," Billy piped in. He had his hearing aids in, so I could tell he had been listening in to our whole conversation.

"I don't know what's wrong with you two," I said crossly. "We came all this way to stop the curse and now it's got a bit more complicated you want to give up. What kind of adventure would that be?"

They were silent.

Billy picked up Arnold from the box bed we had made earlier and stroked him.

"Arnold isn't sure about Helga," he said quietly. "She tried to throw a shoe at him. And he wonders if it would be so bad if we went home."

"There *is* no home, remember?" I said. "It fell into a big hole in the ground. But maybe if we stop the curse, we could go back. Mum could go back to the job she loves and she and Dad would stop arguing because they wouldn't have to worry about us all the time and we wouldn't have to move school and things could go back to the way they were." I remembered my dream and how good it had felt. A lump rose in my throat.

"It's just that Arnold—"

"Arnold doesn't have a say in this," I snapped. "He's a ferret and it's time you grew up."

"Fine," Billy said.

He wriggled back down into his green sleeping bag. He looked like a very grumpy caterpillar, but I wasn't in the mood for finding him funny.

Neena put a hand gently on his arm. "If you feel something strongly, Billy, then you need to talk for yourself."

He swallowed. "Do you think it's a good plan, Neena?" he asked at last.

I looked at Neena pleadingly.

"I do, if Noah does," Neena said.

Billy sniffed and hugged Arnold tighter. He had spent so much of his life afraid. Like in the back of the car on that first night we had moved to Verity Close, whilst being chased by the birds. And again, when I had pulled him from the bathtub of our collapsed house. It made me want to wrap him in my arms and protect him from everything. Because I was his big brother. But I knew in order to stop the curse and have a chance of getting our lives back, we were all going to have to take some risks.

"I just need you to be brave one more time," I said gently. "Can you do that?"

Billy looked at me and Neena again, and then nodded.

# CHAPTER 33

It was nine a.m. and we were on the beach. There were a few people settling down with their beach towels. But nobody seemed to notice when Helga snapped open her huge carpetbag on the sand. Inside the bag Helga had packed all the things we needed: the lantern, a pair of binoculars and a pirate flag we had bought from a shop on the way down. The fire poker lay in the bottom of the bag too.

"We should keep all the gifts together," Helga said.

I pulled the door knocker out of my pocket and handed it over. Helga took it from me, her hands shaking, and laid it gently in the bottom of the bag. I could see a wave of emotion flicker over her face before she snapped the case closed.

"We're so nearly there," she said. "Just one more object — and then we'll be free." She glanced at me. "Think of that, Noah."

Helga lifted the binoculars to her eyes. She peered through them before nodding.

"I think this is a good spot, don't you?" Helga said, passing the binoculars over to me.

I peered through them. Helga was right. From where we stood, we could see the coach stop. It wasn't far from the beach, just a little way up a hilly slope, with the perfect vantage point of the beach. If there was to be a huge commotion down here, people would stop and stare.

"I need to be down there," Helga said, pointing to the cove at the other end of the beach, "so I can control the tide without anyone seeing me. Billy, you're in the car park, waiting for the coach to pull in. Neena and Noah, you need to be here with the binoculars so you can give me a signal for when you see Mr Grey get off the coach and again when Billy's got the case."

Neena hopped up on a nearby bench with the binoculars, and I joined her with the pirate flag. I gave a thumbs up to Helga.

"Ready," I said.

"Now, Billy, when everyone's distracted, you

sneak up to the coach and grab Mr Grey's bag," Helga said.

"But can't I be lookout or help with the lantern?" he said.

Despite gulping down two ice cream sandwiches that morning, he was looking very pale. Helga glanced at me nervously. I crouched down and put my hands on his shoulders.

"We talked about this," I said gently. "You're the only one of us small enough to climb into the hold to grab Mr Grey's suitcase. Plus, I know how good you are at hiding. No one will see you."

"That's right," said Helga encouragingly, lifting the lantern. "Everyone will be too busy watching the show to notice you. When you have the bag, you meet us back at the cove."

I looked at Billy worriedly. Without his help this would never work. But Billy gave me a glimmer of a smile and signed, "Got you, brother."

"I can see a coach arriving," Neena shouted to us.

"OK!" Helga called. She sounded giddy with excitement. "We can do this, team. Places, please."

Helga did a little hoppy run down to the cove, clutching the bag, and Billy huddled behind the ice cream hut with us. Neena and I passed the binoculars back and forth, frantically trying to spot Mr Grey amongst the passengers.

"What if he's not there?" Neena said.

"He'll be there," I said. "He has to be there."

And then, right at the back of a coach pulling into the stop, I spotted a shock of white-blond hair at the window. I picked up the pirate flag and waved it triumphantly. A few moments passed and the passengers started to get off the coach. But nothing was happening. I frowned. Maybe Helga hadn't seen our signal. I waved the pirate flag again. But nothing happened. The sea remained glassy and still. Everyone was beginning to get off the coach. But Billy couldn't make a break for the coach hold unless Helga came through with her distraction. I felt a knot in my stomach as I thought of all the things that could have gone wrong. Maybe the matches had got wet and wouldn't light? Maybe Helga couldn't get the lantern to work? Maybe Helga had thought the plan was too dangerous after all? But then, just as the coach driver opened the hold, there was an almighty roar and then a crash as the waves suddenly raced up the beach. Then the waves began to grow. Getting bigger and bigger, until the ocean became one almighty towering wave. It broke just over our heads, drenching both me and Neena. I didn't care though, because I could hear the screams and gasps of people on the pier and see the sunbathers running back up the beach. And everyone from the coach was rushing down from the coach stop to see what was going on. Even Mr Grey had joined the bewildered crowd. And I could see Billy breaking cover and running to the coach.

I watched Billy ducking and darting and pushing his way through the crowd until he was at the coach. He hesitated a moment before diving into the hold.

"Come on. Come on," I muttered.

The lantern's powers were waning. The sea slipped back from the foreshore and the crowd began to disperse. Just then, Neena gave a little whoop of glee. She passed me the binoculars and I could see Billy, clutching the suitcase tight to his chest.

But I could see Mr Grey too, turning in the crowd, as though he had suddenly realized the danger. Pushing his way back through towards the coach.

"Run!" I shouted, even though Billy couldn't hear me. "Run!"

But the crowd was dispersing, and Billy was losing his cover. It didn't take Mr Grey long to spot him.

"Hey!" he roared, his voice so loud we could catch it on the wind. "Thief!"

The coach crowd began to murmur. A couple of passengers reached out to catch Billy. But Billy was sprinting now. Ducking and diving through people's arms and legs. Mr Grey was pushing his way after him. Knocking people down. There were shouts and screams from the crowd. Billy yelled "Help!" as Mr Grey's fingers grazed the back of his collar. I watched through the binoculars helplessly. Someone reached out to catch Mr Grey's arm. It was Pat the ice cream lady who had served us yesterday.

"Leave that little kid alone!" she yelled.

Her interruption was all Billy needed. He pelted back down the beach.

But Mr Grey had shaken off Pat and was close on his heels. And then Billy tripped. And the bag, Billy and Mr Grey were all tangled up together and tumbling along the beachfront. Neena and I broke cover and ran full pelt at Mr Grey.

"Get off my brother!" I roared.

Mr Grey looked up, holding his hand out to stop us. But me and Neena didn't stop. Just before we all collided, I grabbed Neena's hand and we swung our arms up together. Our fists hit him squarely in the stomach. There was a little *oof* sound. And Mr Grey crumpled on the ground, clutching his bag.

"Go," I shouted to Billy, as Neena dived on to Mr Grey. "Get back to Helga."

"Stop!" Mr Grey growled. He shook Neena

off and staggered to his feet. He caught hold of my T-shirt. "Listen to me, boy, you need to hear me," he hissed.

But there was a crowd forming around us, with Pat as their leader. She stepped forward, her hands on her hips.

"I said leave those kids alone."

Mr Grey let go of my T-shirt.

"It's not what it looks like," he stammered. "They had my bag."

Pat didn't blink.

"Well, now you've got it back," she said coldly. "So, beat it."

Mr Grey glanced at us for a moment, before taking her advice. Turning, he pushed his way through the crowd, taking the precious weathervane with him.

# CHAPTER 34

It took us ages to get away from the concerned crowd on the beach. Everyone wanted to know what was going on. If we were all right? If Billy was hurt? It took Neena reassuring everyone several times we were really were fine before they would leave us alone. But even then, Pat insisted on walking us back to Helga's.

"We really ought to report this. Can't have men like that going around assaulting little kids. But at the very least you should let me walk you back to your granny's," she said.

"Really, it's OK, we're meeting Helga on the beach, and she'll know what to do," Neena said again.

Pat didn't look very convinced but eventually she let us go.

But, by the time we made it to the sheltered cove, neither Billy nor Helga was anywhere to be seen.

Neena frowned.

"Where are they?" she said. "Where did they go?"

"Maybe they went back to Helga's?" I said, starting to feel panicky.

"But they know it's not safe. Mr Grey knows where Helga lives. It will be the first place he'll go now, and they know that."

"Maybe we should go and see," I said. "I'm sure Helga will know the right thing to do. She's probably come up with a new plan."

Neena looked at me.

"Maybe," she said hesitantly.

We got back to Helga's and cautiously opened the door. We went in quietly and called softly up the stairs, then searched each room. Arnold was still asleep in a cardboard box. Neither Helga nor Billy were anywhere to be seen.

"Look," hissed Neena, clutching my arm. I followed her gaze and saw there was a note pinned to the armchair.

Neena snatched it up.

*The boy for the gift. The clifftops at dusk.*

And then, out from the shadows of the kitchen, stepped Mr Grey.

"I think it's time we had that talk now," he said.

Neena and I exchanged one terrified look, before bolting for the front door.

"Wait!" Mr Grey bellowed. "If you want to get your brother back, then stop."

My hand froze at the door handle. I turned slowly.

"Where's Billy? What have you done with him?" I said, curling my hands into fists.

"I don't have him, but if you want him back," Mr Grey said, putting his hands up, "you're going to have to trust me."

"Oh yeah, and why should we do that?" I said.

"Because," Mr Grey said, removing his glasses and lifting his fringe from his forehead to reveal the same startling green eyes that me, Billy, Mum and Helga all shared, "I'm a Bradley."

# CHAPTER 35

I felt like my voice had flown out of my body because all I could do was gape open-mouthed at Mr Grey. And the more I looked at Mr Grey, the more I could see it. It had been there all along, the shiver of recognition I'd felt in the hospital. The thing I couldn't put my finger on when we had fought in the house. It wasn't just the shimmery green eyes. It was the high cheekbones, wide mouth and the hint of red that came through underneath his shock of white hair – all this time he'd reminded me of Mum.

Neena found her voice first. "I don't understand," she said. "If you're a Bradley, why have you been trying to steal the door knocker?"

He sank down into the armchair and rubbed his

forehead. "I haven't been trying to steal it. I've been trying to stop Helga getting it."

"Why?" I asked.

"*Until, united again with their true strength, they could bring the curse to a close,*" he said softly. "That's the legend, isn't it? And that's what Helga told your mother — that the objects united could break the curse. But she's wrong."

"What?" I said.

He smiled in a tired sort of way. "Even at their most powerful, our objects cannot stop the birds. Or the accidents that follow us. They didn't before and they cannot again."

I sat down heavily on one of Helga's boxes. It crushed, giving way to my full weight. But I barely noticed. Everything I had believed had fallen apart and I was scrambling to put the pieces back together.

"But what does it mean?" I asked. "*United again with their true strength.* That must mean the gifts."

Mr Grey bent down in front of me. I could see my own strange green eyes reflected back in his thick glasses.

"It doesn't mean the gifts, Noah; it means us. Our family," Mr Grey said softly.

I frowned. "I don't understand," I said.

"Helga conveniently focused on the last part of the

legend. But there's more, isn't there? *They cursed the family to be rootless as they once were, chased by the birds of the north, who would bring misfortune to any place they came to call home for so long as they held on to magic.* It's the magic, Noah. The magic made our family weak and selfish. To break the curse, we need to unite and show that together we have the strength to do what we couldn't back then."

"To do what?" I asked.

"Destroy the gifts. So they can never be misused again."

Neena sat down heavily beside me, making another box collapse in on itself. But she didn't seem to notice either.

"Of course," she said, shaking her head like she'd been terribly stupid. "You can't break a curse by repeating the same mistake."

"But if all this is true," I said, "why did you kidnap Billy?"

He stared at me for a moment. "I didn't kidnap Billy," he said quietly.

"Then who—" But Neena broke off before she could finish her sentence.

She reached over and gripped my hand, shaking.

"Oh, Noah, you were right back in the cave! Helga did come up with a new plan," she said.

A slow, horrible realization began to dawn on me. The note wasn't for us. It was for Mr Grey. She had kidnapped Billy to force him to give up the weathervane.

"But why?" I said.

"Because she wants their power. Always has. Always will," Mr Grey said. "How do you think she got to be in possession of two of the gifts?"

I thought back to Helga's letter. How she had said someone was hunting us for what we had. But now I knew it wasn't Mr Grey. It was always Helga. And now she had my little brother. I could feel the room begin to spin. I blinked away little colourful spots, and backed up against the wall, trying to steady myself.

"Noah, are you all right?" Neena asked.

"It's all my fault," I mumbled. Mum and Dad made me promise to protect Billy. And I hadn't listened. I could feel my insides tighten like a boa constrictor was wrapping itself around my guts.

"No it isn't," Neena said, grabbing both my shoulders and shaking me.

"We'll give Helga what she wants and get Billy back, won't we?" she said, glancing over at Mr Grey.

Mr Grey leaned back so heavily into the old armchair that he knocked the stuffing out of the pillows. The room filled with silence and soft white feathers.

"Helga wants this," he said, pulling the weathervane from his suitcase. It was an old brass cross with compass points. But even though it didn't look like anything special, I knew how powerful the other magic objects were. I watched it warily as it glinted in the light from the window.

"She has all the others, doesn't she?"

I thought of how I had handed over the door knocker to Helga without thinking twice, and shivered.

"So, with this weathervane, Helga will have the full power of the gifts. And that would be a dangerous and terrible thing," he finished. "All of that power, controlling the land, the animals in it, the sea, the thunder and lightning, even the stars."

I shook my head.

"Giving it to her is the only way I can get Billy back!" I said.

"We won't abandon him," Neena joined in fiercely.

"Of course not," Mr Grey said. "Knowing what Helga is capable of, I couldn't leave your brother in her hands. But before we make this decision we must think carefully," Mr Grey said, before mumbling, "Perhaps there is another way."

Mr Grey flicked the compass points on the weathervane until they spun slightly, making the air crackle with electricity. Then he bent forward in the chair, resting his head in his hands. His heavy fringe flopped back over his eyes. Neena and I looked at each other anxiously. The minutes ticked away. The room filled with a heavy silence, only broken by a very faint tapping on the window.

*Tap. Tap. Tap.*

As time ticked on, it grew louder and louder.

*Tap. Tap. Tap.*

"I'm trying to think," muttered Mr Grey.

*Tap. Tap. Tap.*

"Will someone stop that noise!" Mr Grey finally roared.

I got up to check the tap in the kitchen, but it wasn't dripping. Then I noticed something at the window. A shadow. I reached out to pull up the blinds.

They snapped open and I froze. My heart skipped a beat and my blood ran cold. Outside, tapping at the frosted glass, was a black bird of the north.

"Is that. . ." Neena started from behind me, her eyes wide.

"A black bird from the north," I said. "Come to drive a Bradley from their home. But it's not for me, or Mr Grey. It's for Helga. They've finally caught up to her."

Mr Grey joined us by the kitchen window.

"But there's only one," Neena said, craning her head out of the window. "I thought they came in a big flock?"

"Sometimes they do. Sometimes, if they've had very far to fly, they send one ahead. The others are never far behind," Mr Grey said. He turned to us and his eyes were gleaming. "The others are never far behind," he repeated softly.

"I think I have an idea," he said. "But it's risky. It's dangerous, and if it doesn't work, it could condemn us to a life cursed for ever."

I thought about how until recently that had been my worst fear. How all I had wanted was to fix the curse. All my problems would go away. I wouldn't have to change schools any more, I could mend my friendships, I could finally be the normal boy I had always tried so hard to be.

But, standing in Helga's living room and filled with the emptiness of losing Billy, I realized how stupid and selfish that all seemed. Because I didn't care about going back to school or being friends with people I realized I didn't even really like. I didn't care about being normal any more. Because normal people didn't get to go on mad adventures with their best friends. And I didn't even care about having a home. Not if I couldn't share it with the person I loved the most.

"I don't care how dangerous it is, or what I might have to give up, I'm getting my brother back," I said finally.

Mr Grey nodded once. "You should leave," he said to Neena. "There's no curse on you and I'd rather not bring you into danger."

"I'm not going anywhere," Neena said, folding her arms.

I looked at the bird outside again. It was watching us with its black beady eyes, its sharp beak following us as we moved around the room. A cold shiver ran down my spine.

"Neena, he's right. You should go," I said.

Neena turned to me, her face full of hurt and confusion.

"You don't mean that," she said.

"You have a home. With people who love you. This isn't your problem any more," I said, looking away from her.

"That's not the reason though, is it?" Neena said, gently putting a hand on my shoulder.

I made a soft circle in the carpet with my toe.

"I can't lose you too," I said quietly. "You're my best friend."

Neena gave my shoulder a firm squeeze.

"Noah Bradley, you promised me an adventure. And we're not done yet," she said.

Mr Grey considered us for a very long time, before letting out a heavy sigh.

"I was afraid you were going to say that," he said.

# CHAPTER 36

The path to the clifftops was steep and rocky. All the way up, I felt the black bear growling and clawing away at my insides. But I needed to be brave. As brave as I'd ever been, for Billy. We passed a quiet church and carried on up until we reached the summit, just as the sun sank below the clifftops. We could see Helga waiting.

She stood close to the edge, one arm locked tightly around Billy's chest, whilst the other hand clutched the fire poker.

"Billy!" I called out, signing desperately, "Are you OK?"

"He's fine," called back Helga. "Let's keep him that way."

The big carpetbag was at her feet. She was flushed with excitement.

"Well, well," she said, smiling. "Hello, all, and welcome to the Bradley family reunion."

"I never was one for parties," Mr Grey said. He took a step forward.

"That's close enough," Helga said, holding out the poker menacingly. "Let me see it," she added, nodding to the suitcase in Mr Grey's hands.

Mr Grey put the suitcase carefully on the ground but didn't let go of it.

"Let go of the boy first," he commanded.

Helga shook her head and tightened her grip on Billy. Billy gave a little yelp.

"Let him go," I cried out.

"Then give me what I came for," Helga said. "And you can have your brother back." Her eyes narrowed. "Have you even brought the weathervane?"

"Yes," I said. I knelt, opened the suitcase and took out the weathervane.

I could feel the familiar buzz in my hands, but this time it was much, much stronger than anything I'd felt before. Even holding it gently I could feel the crackle of lightning in the air. Down below, the sea began to stir. Crashing against the cliffs as the wind began to howl.

"Good," Helga said softly. "Now hand it over." Her face was lit with determination.

My eyes looked to the horizon, straining to see. But the light had faded fast, and Helga was running out of patience. The fire poker in her hand was spitting out little blue flames.

"Just tell me one thing," I said, trying to keep my voice calm. "What are you planning to do with the gifts once you have them?"

Helga smiled, her eyes on the weathervane. Now that it was nearly in her grasp, she seemed to relax slightly.

"Whatever I want," she said, her lip curling meanly.

"But then the curse will never be broken," said Mr Grey. "Even with all the power in the world, you'll still be running for ever."

"What is safety and security without power? I can live in a new house every year. A beach hut in Barbados, a town house in Paris, a castle in Scotland."

"Cousin, this isn't right," Mr Grey said. "We Bradleys were cursed for our selfishness. We're not meant to have these gifts. No one is."

"*Right!*" Helga spat. "Was it *right* for us to spend our lives cursed for something our ancestors did?"

"We can't change the past," I yelled over the sound of the wind and the crashing of the waves below. "We can only change the future."

"Enough! Give it to me," Helga said.

I thought of all the bad and selfish things I had done in the past. Lying about who I was. Making fun of people just so that Jackson would like me. Putting my family in danger again and again, because I was only thinking of myself. I couldn't change any of those things. But I knew I didn't want to be that person any more. I wanted to be a new Noah – or maybe the old one, who had been there all along. A Noah who deserved Neena Kapoor as a friend. A Noah who looked after his little brother no matter what. A Noah who was true to himself. I wanted to be *that* person, even if our plan failed and I had to stay cursed for ever.

And I heard it then. The faintest *thump thump thump*, so distant I could barely hear it.

I stepped forward with the weathervane.

"Don't do it, Noah," Billy said bravely. "Don't give it to her."

But my mind was made up. I glanced at Mr Grey, who gave me a small nod.

"Take it," I said, throwing it on the ground between us. "Just give me my brother back."

"Well, thank you," Helga said, her catlike smile reappearing as she scooped it up. She released Billy. "Go on, boy."

Billy ran to me and I hugged him tight. And again on the breeze, I heard it. The soft *thump, thump* of wings.

Helga didn't notice; she was too busy packing away the door knocker into her large carpetbag. She straightened up and smiled at us.

"I think this brings our little reunion to an end," she said, waving the poker at us to clear a path.

"Wait!" Neena said, jumping in front of Helga. The flame from the poker caught her cheek, but Neena didn't flinch. "Before you leave, don't you want to try it?"

Helga lowered the poker, just a little.

"Try what?" she asked curiously.

"The gifts," Neena said, her voice eager. "Together they have their full strength now, right?"

"Well, I'm not so sure about that," Mr Grey said mildly, turning to us. "Some say their true power was broken when we were cursed. Some say that even united they are but worthless objects, capable only of raising a few waves and the odd spark."

Helga frowned.

"Oh, no, cousin," she said coldly. "Shall I show

you how very wrong you are?" And she pulled out the lantern from her bag. I could feel a hum coming off it. Just like I'd felt a hum when I'd handed over the weathervane.

Helga drew a slim box of matches from his pocket and struck the wick in the lantern. A small flame leapt and flickered.

"The lantern that can summon the sea!" Helga yelled as she waved it across the clifftops.

Below us, the sea began to surge and heave. Helga cackled. Because it was nothing like the few waves she had managed to summon earlier. Now the sea was a raging typhoon. It grew bigger and bigger, until finally Helga blew out the light and it all crashed down into a big, dark, churning whirlpool. We all gasped. But it wasn't the sea I was watching any more. Behind us on the horizon I could see a fast-moving black cloud. I couldn't help a slow grin spreading across my face.

"And now," Helga said, "after that little demonstration, I think I'll be taking my leave." She stopped. "Why are you smiling, boy?" she asked.

"Because, even with all that power," I said, pointing to her bag, "there's still one thing you can't control."

"Really?" Helga said. "And what's that?"

But none of us had to answer. Because suddenly the air was filled with the unmistakable, haunting cry of the black birds of the north.

# CHAPTER 37

Helga took a step back. Her expression had changed from gloating pleasure to one of frozen fear. There was no escape. Not for Helga at least. The birds were coming for her, and she knew it.

"You're trapped," Billy said gleefully, finally understanding our plan.

"But united we can end this curse," I said. "So, help us."

"How?" Helga said, trembling.

"Four Bradleys and four magical objects. To be united, we must each destroy one," Mr Grey said, reaching out for the carpetbag still clutched in Helga's shaking hand. "Please, Helga. We must each throw these into the sea. Free us all from this terrible curse."

But Helga stepped back, clasping the carpetbag to her chest and waving the poker before her, creating great swirling arcs of blue fire.

"There must be another way," she stammered.

"There isn't," Mr Grey said. "It must be this. We have to hurry."

The great *thump, thump, thump* of a thousand wings in the air grew closer. I saw the terror in Helga's eyes. She wasn't the monster who had tricked us or stolen my brother. She was just a woman who, over the years, had lost more and more until she had lost herself.

"Helga," I said, "it's not too late for friends or family."

I reached out for her hand. But the fear had left Helga's eyes, only to be replaced with something else, something I didn't like at all. She pulled out the weathervane.

"I'll strike them down with wind and lightning!" she cried.

She forced the weathervane high into the sky against the wind. The compass points spun, and I could hear a tremendous roar, just before a great gust of air swept over the hilltop. It bent the trees and knocked us all from our feet.

I scrambled up again to see the birds swoop in over the church spire we had passed on our way up.

The wind wasn't stopping them or even slowing them down. Helga rose to her feet and lifted the weathervane to the air again, and this time it spun frantically in the other direction. The hair on the end of my neck and my arms stood up. Lightning bolts tumbled down from the sky, hitting the earth with such force that every strike left a great steaming crater.

"Get down!" Mr Grey bellowed.

I pulled Billy to the ground and flung myself over him. Mr Grey and Neena threw herself down beside us. The lightning buzzed overhead, but still the birds came. I reached out and grabbed Neena's hand. She squeezed it back.

"There has to be something I can use to stop them," Helga cried. She dropped the weathervane and pulled out the lantern.

The sky above screeched with a thousand cries of the black birds of the north. As they passed over us, I could feel the velvety tips of their wings, the beats of air, the clip of talons. I saw Helga raise a match. And then I heard her scream.

They were on her. Their talons and beaks tore at her hands and clothes. Helga screamed again as they dive-bombed over and over. Soon the bag was torn from her hands, before, with a final swoop, the birds carried Helga off towards the clifftop edge. Only then did Helga drop the lantern. I pulled myself to the cliff edge just in time to see it smash on the rocks below and Helga disappear under the waves.

But the birds did not pause. They turned, and they came again. Because there were still more Bradleys, and now they would come for us all.

"The bag," I yelled.

Billy snatched it up.

"We need to get to cover," I said, pointing to the thin strip of trees at the far side of the clifftop.

Neena and I pulled Billy to his feet and we began to run, Mr Grey close behind us. I could feel sharp beaks jabbing the back of my neck, the top of my head, as huge talons raked across my arms. I wanted to yell out in pain, but the air was so thick with birds, I could hardly breathe. Finally, we made it into the thin thicket of trees and brambles. The birds flew over, their shrieks fading away. But they would be back; our cover wouldn't last long.

"What now?" Neena panted, rubbing a trickle of blood from her forehead.

"The only way to stop them is to destroy the gifts," Mr Grey said grimly. "We need to throw them into the sea; it's the only thing powerful enough to break them."

I peered out from the bushes only to see the birds

circling back over the clifftops. They turned in the air like one dark wave.

"I don't think we'll make it," I said, trembling.

"Then we'll die trying," Neena said firmly, but I could hear the fear in her voice.

We all got to our feet, tensing ourselves for the deadly dash across the clifftop. Mr Grey gave us a nod, but before I could take a step forward, Billy ripped the bag from my hands.

"Wait!" he yelled. "I've a better idea," he finished breathlessly, pulling the fire poker from the bag.

Billy lifted the poker. Blue fire sprang up, bigger and bigger, until it was the size of a bonfire and we all backed away.

"The fire's magic, it'll be able to destroy them," Billy said before the sky was once again filled with the cries of the black birds of the north.

"We have to hurry!" I said, passing Mr Grey the weathervane.

Mr Grey turned it lovingly in his hands one last time, before letting it drop into the fire. It crackled for a moment before bursting into blue sparks and vanishing. The blue flames grew bigger and brighter.

"Now you," I said to Billy.

Billy tossed the poker, without hesitation, into the flames. The fire rose still higher, crackling frantically.

Finally, I pulled the door knocker from the bag. Just for a moment, I hesitated. It had been in our family for generations. It had survived hundreds of moves. We had spent so long protecting it, and I could still feel its magic. It felt powerful, like the way I had with my friends at school. I wondered if that was why Helga couldn't let the lantern go until it was too late.

"Noah," said Neena. She squeezed my arm. "Let it go."

With a deep breath I threw the door knocker into the flames. With a whoosh, the fire exploded into a roaring bonfire. The fox face glowed, before, with an almighty crackle, it melted away.

For just a moment after, the whole world seemed to freeze. It was as though a heaviness I didn't know I had was lifted out of me. And then all around us the black birds from the north fell from the sky.

As they hit the ground, they disappeared into nothing more than ash. The last of the curse vanished, drifting like smoke up into the starry sky.

# CHAPTER 38

I couldn't remember much of what had happened after the birds had disappeared. But apparently me, Billy and Mr Grey all collapsed. Neena had gone back into town to get help and found Pat, who had driven us all to the hospital, before very kindly going to back to Cliff Top Cottage to rescue Arnold.

They told me in the hospital afterwards that I had slept for nearly two days. I guess running away, finding out you have two long-lost relatives, and fighting one of them, not to mention breaking a long-standing family curse, can really take it out of you. I was covered in scratches, cuts and bruises from our battle with the black birds of the north. But none of it mattered because I could *feel* it. A lightness in my chest. Everything was different; everything had changed. From my hospital window the sky was clear and beside me was Billy. He had bandaged hands but was grinning ear to ear like he knew the most tremendous secret. And leaning over my bed was Mum, and holding her hand was Dad.

"We did it. Didn't we?" I asked sleepily.

Mum stoked my head, tears in her eyes. "You did. You really did," she said.

There was so much more to say. So many questions to ask. Were we in trouble? Would Dad stay with us? Where would we live? But I was still so tired.

"Sleep now," Dad said as he brushed my hair back from my eyes.

And, for the first time in for ever, I fell back to sleep without a worry chasing through my dreams.

The next time I woke up, Mr Grey was standing over me.

I wasn't sure how I felt about Mr Grey now. We had spent so long being afraid of him that it was hard seeing him as a friend.

"Why didn't you tell us everything when we first met?" I asked.

"I should have done," he said. "I should have tried in the hospital that day. But I couldn't risk you not helping me. I knew that no matter what I had to get the gift off you, to save it falling into Helga's hands. And then I realized Helga had been writing to your mum and I knew I had to get to her before you did."

"And so you went after her?"

Mr Grey nodded. "Once she had the door knocker, it would only be me standing between her and all the power she had ever dreamed of. She would never stop, and I was getting too old to outrun her," he said. "I thought it was time this all ended."

I thought of Helga being swept off the cliff by the black birds of the north. Her head disappearing beneath the waves. Maybe she had been able to survive the fall and swim to safety. Mr Grey seemed to guess what I was thinking.

"She won't be coming back, Noah," Mr Grey said.

And even after all she'd done, I felt a sort of sadness.

"What will you do now the curse is broken?" I asked.

Mr Grey shrugged. "I don't know. I never really thought about what would happen after," he said. "But us Bradleys should keep in touch, now there are so few of us left."

Then he reached into his big leather suitcase and pulled out a huge, spiky cactus.

"Housewarming present. I've a feeling you'll be needing it soon," he said, with a wink.

Then the day came when we had to leave hospital and return home. Only there wasn't one to go to. 18 Verity Close was gone. Dad told me it was going to be knocked down and made into an allotment. The thought made my heart hurt a little. But a part of me was glad too. It meant all of us could start over again. Somewhere new, somewhere that could be all of ours. In the meantime, Dad rented us a room in a cheap B & B in Hockley. But when we arrived back in Hockley all the questions began. I had thought breaking an ancient family curse was exhausting, but this was even worse. Every day there seemed to be someone new who needed to know what had happened. Mr and Mrs Kapoor wanted to know the full story, of course. They had been so kind, and I wanted to tell them the truth, but it also seemed impossible. It was the kind of story you could only believe if you had been there.

So, we let Neena do most of the talking. She told them it was her idea to run away. And then they wanted to know why. Neena explained how miserable she had been feeling. How she felt like she could never talk about the way she was feeling or how much she missed Jasmin. How she wanted to remember her sister and look at photos of her. And how everything at school was awful too. Hearing Neena talk about how miserable my friends had made her and how I had

been a part of that filled me with shame. Mr and Mrs
Kapoor were angry and sad and then very, very quiet.
But when it came time for Mum, Dad, Billy and me
to leave, Mrs Kapoor gave me a hug.

"I'm not happy about what you three did," she said.
"But I am happy that Neena has a friend like you."

All I could do was stare at my feet. Because it was
me who was happy to have a friend like Neena.

Then there were questions from the police. They
wanted to know what had happened to us up on the
clifftops. When I tried to explain that a flock of birds
had attacked us, and all three of us stuck to the same
story, it caused an even bigger stir. We had newspapers
calling us and they asked their own questions. They
even ran a story in the local newspaper.

*The Birds – For Real*

*Hike Goes Wrong for Three Runaways*

*Local Woman Missing After Bird Attack*

And then there was Sandra Kim, our social worker.
She had been worried when we had all disappeared.

283

And she had her own questions. She wanted to know exactly why I'd run away. So I ended up telling her a version of the truth. I said that after our house came down and Mum was hospitalized and then we had the break-in, I couldn't stop worrying. And my friends at school were being horrible to me. And that I thought by running away I could keep Billy and me safe from all the terrible things that kept happening. And even though it wasn't the real story, a lot of it was the truth.

It felt so weird and scary talking to someone about all the things I tried to keep stuffed deep down inside of me. Afterwards, I was worried I'd made everything worse. That maybe Miss Kim would think my parents were doing a bad job and take me away. That maybe Mum and Dad would be disappointed in me, or that everyone would think there was something wrong with me. But nobody did. Miss Kim was very kind. She said I'd gone through a lot recently. And that it was important to talk about these things. She even decided it would be a good idea for me to see a counsellor at school, which sounded scary, because:

1. I wasn't sure I wanted to talk to anyone about any of this.
2. Now that I knew I didn't want to be friends with Jackson any more, I wasn't sure I

wanted to go back to school.

But even though we didn't know where we were
going to live yet, and I was still covered in scratches
and bruises, Mum and Dad insisted me and Billy
finish out the last few days of the school term. And
that was when I realized just how much things had
changed.

# CHAPTER 39

I felt the old familiar growl in the pit of my stomach as me and Billy walked to school. I saw Neena waiting for us at the gate. But Mr and Mrs Kapoor were nowhere to be seen.

"Where are your parents?" I asked.

"They thought after all our adventures, I could handle walking to school on my own," Neena said, smiling.

She pulled out a new phone from her pocket.

"They are, however, checking in on me every hour. But I think I can get it down to every two hours by the end of the week."

The school bell rang, and Billy went off to join his junior class. I watched him show off the new mermaid backpack that Mum and Dad had brought him. He was dancing about, showing it off and not caring what anyone thought, and I saw that the other kids were laughing along with him. As I watched, I realized that Billy had been fine all along. It was me, with my jungle rules, too scared of not fitting in, who had needed help.

"Are you ready?" Neena asked.

I thought of how scary it was going to school as the new Noah, the one who didn't follow the jungle rules. The one who just tried to be himself. I didn't know what Jackson, Dylan and Liam were going to think of me.

"Not really," I sighed, following Neena into our form room.

As soon as I walked in, I knew something had shifted in our little classroom jungle. Jackson and Dylan were no longer sitting at the big table at the back, surveying their kingdom. They were sitting up front, at the very worst table right next to Mr Townsend's desk. Both refused to look at me as Neena and I walked past. And then I saw Liam sitting alone by the window at a table for three. He grinned when he saw me.

"Hey," he said. "Sit here?"

We paused.

"Won't your friends mind?" Neena said uncertainly.

"Oh," Liam said awkwardly, glancing at Jackson and Dylan. "We're not really friends any more."

"Why?" I asked, puzzled.

"I hated it when they said you weren't in our history project," Liam said, flushing. "You did all the hard work – it wasn't fair. And I knew all the jokes Jackson made about you were mean, even if I did join in a bit," he added, glancing up at Neena nervously. "I felt terrible after you two disappeared, so I ended up telling Miss Ackerly everything." He bit his lip. "Well, nearly everything," he said, and me and Neena knew he was talking about the door knocker.

"Well, in that case," Neena said, throwing her bag down, "you better budge up."

We took our seats as Mr Townsend came around to collect phones. Liam gave his up without even trying to hide it.

"How are things with your mum?" I asked.

"Better, thanks," he said, adding, "She was just asking about you too. Said you should come to our big summer BBQ. It might not be as good as last year though, because Dad's not allowed to do fireworks again."

"Why not?" I asked.

"He nearly blew up the cat last time," Liam said. "But if you're asking me, that was the best bit."

I grinned; I knew how much Liam loved explosions.

"If you're looking for something to go bang, I think there's a bit in here about how to make gunpowder," Neena said, pulling out a book with the title *Historical Crimes and Murders*.

Liam gave her an impressed look, then said, "Really? Cool," as they began to flick through the pages together.

Everything only got better from there. Miss Ackerly had even had the cup engraved with my name on it. It stood proudly on her desk with my name there, Noah Bradley, for all to see. She even made everyone give me a little clap at the start of class. The funny thing was that as much as it made me proud, it wasn't even the best part of my day. The best bit ended up being walking back home with Liam, Neena and Billy, listening to Billy talk about what he'd been doing in school.

"Did you know that there's an octopus that's literally immortal? When it gets old it shrivels up and then gets reborn as a larva and starts all over again," he said happily.

"Whoa, I wonder what's that like?" Liam said.

Billy gave me a small smile. We had started over so many times, it felt like we already knew.

# CHAPTER 40

A week into the school holidays, as Billy and I were watching TV in our room at the B & B, Mum and Dad came back with what they said was good news.

"We found a place," Mum said. "A home!"

"Near Verity Close?" I asked.

"It's a little outside town. In fact, it's in a nearby village."

My heart sank. I didn't want to change schools again — not now that I had made a proper friend. Two friends, including Liam.

"But I don't want to leave my school," I said.

"That's the best part," Mum said, grinning. "I talked to Mr Hoad and we all agreed it would be best if you carried on at St Jude's. It means you'll have to get a bus in, but getting up early never hurt anyone. I can carry on at the restaurant too."

I couldn't believe it; a new home *and* I didn't have to change schools. It all seemed too good to be true. I looked at Dad.

"What about your work?" I asked.

"Well." He smiled at Mum. "Your mum and I thought it was time I took a job a little closer to home. So, I'll be starting as a construction site manager in town."

"But that's not making big exciting buildings," Billy piped in. "You love that."

"I think I've had enough excitement for a lifetime. And this new job means I'll be home for tea, every night," Dad said.

"It means he'll be *making* your tea," Mum added, laughing. "I'll be working late a lot. But it'll be worth it."

Mum was beaming. Everyone at her job at the restaurant had been really nice to us; they had sent us all trays and trays of food and given Mum lots of time off work to heal and go house hunting. But I could tell she couldn't wait to get back to work again.

"What does it look like?" Billy asked, jumping on to the end of the bed. "The new house?"

"Well, it's smaller than Verity Close," Mum said, putting an arm around him.

"And it's not exactly a house," Dad added.

I wondered if it would be another trailer, or a camper van. But if it meant I got to stay at school, and we all got to stay together, I didn't really mind too much.

"Will we have our own rooms?" Billy asked.

"Yes," Mum said. "Definitely."

Billy made a little whooping sound and swept Arnold up into his arms.

"Hear that, Arnold? We get our very own room," he said, dancing around the room with Arnold.

"Good, no more ferrets in my bed," I said.

Dad laughed and scratched behind Arnold's ears.

"We're renting it from a woman who's moving abroad next week," Mum said. "She says it's ours for as long as we want it."

"For ever?" I asked.

"If we like," Mum said, looking at Dad.

"For a very long time, at least," Dad said.

"Anyway, don't think I've forgotten about our tradition," Mum said, and from her handbag she pulled a tourist map and brochure of our new village.

*The Wonders of Bamford*, it read.

I thought of all the other maps I'd kept over the years. Maps of other countries and towns and cities. Maps of places we'd left in the middle of the night, or early in the morning. Maps of places we hadn't stayed in long enough to explore. Maps of places I'd been glad to leave and ones I hadn't.

I opened this one gently. I wanted to take in everything about my new home, which might even be a forever home. I looked at the parks and the little museum and even the historical buildings. But then I saw something that made me smile.

"Anything you think we should check out?" Mum asked.

I nodded.

"There's something here we should definitely see. But I need to bring someone with us," I said.

I was buzzing with excitement when Dad's van pulled up outside Neena's house. Neena and her parents were waiting outside for us on the little wall. Mum went to say hello to Mrs Kapoor; they were still the best of friends.

"Perhaps you'd like to come with us too?" Mum asked Mrs Kapoor.

"Oh, that's all right," Mrs Kapoor said, glancing at Neena. They'd been trying hard to give her independence. "We can hear all about it when Neena gets back."

"You should come," I said suddenly. "I'd think you'd like it too."

"Where exactly are we going?" Neena asked as we clambered into the van.

"It's a surprise," I said.

"He won't even tell me," Billy said.

Mr and Mrs Kapoor followed behind us in their Mini. We drove through the city until we arrived at the big white building that was the village museum. Neena raised an eyebrow.

"A museum? After another history cup already, are you?"

"Just wait and see," I said, enjoying the mystery.

We walked into the foyer, past the big exhibits and right to the back, to a dark corridor.

"Close your eyes," I said to Neena. "Keep them closed till I tell you to open them."

"Noah!" She groaned, but she shut her eyes tight.

I guided her through the corridor and out into a big old Victorian greenhouse. Her parents followed, and then Mum and Dad and Billy. The glass ceiling arched above us like a huge bell. The light filtered in, casting rainbows across our arms. And all around us hundreds of butterflies filled the air.

"Open your eyes," I said.

Slowly, she did so, and then she gasped.

"Noah!" she said. "Where are we?"

"It's a butterfly house," I said. "I thought it was

somewhere you could come when you were missing your sister."

For the first time since I had known Neena, she was speechless. All she could do was smile as we watched butterflies of every colour float around us. And then the smallest white butterfly landed on Neena's finger.

"You know the amazing thing about butterflies?" I asked Neena.

Neena shook her head.

"Some butterflies live for a whole year; some only live for a day. But even though they're gone, they've still helped make all of *this*." I pointed at the flowers. "So you can never forget them."

We all watched in silence as Neena lifted her hand and let the white butterfly go. It spiralled up, up into the dome, until it was out of sight. For a moment Neena's hand stayed frozen, outstretched. And then Mrs Kapoor took it.

"You know, the first time your sister saw a butterfly, she was terrified," Mrs Kapoor said.

"Really?" Neena said, wiping her nose.

"She had fallen asleep in the garden and when she woke up, she was covered in them."

"You never heard a child scream so loud," Mr Kapoor added, smiling.

"I don't know why, but somehow I can't imagine her little," Neena said.

"We have lots of pictures. It has been hard for us to look at them, but maybe it is time we showed them to you," Mrs Kapoor said.

We left Neena and her parents on the bench amongst the ferns and tall plants. One by one the butterflies came to land next to them. But they didn't seem to notice. They were too busy talking.

# CHAPTER 41

Two weeks later we all jumbled into Dad's van. Billy sat in the back with Arnold. Mum sat in the front. She winced when she pulled the seatbelt on, but she was no longer reaching for the painkillers or icepacks. My and Billy's cuts and scratches had all faded too. But even so, Dad refused to let anyone help with the packing of the van. Dad had managed to save a few things from our house, including my broken bike. So, the van filled up quickly. He ended up having to strap Mum's trunk to the roof.

"Done," he said, panting, after a few sweary moments.

Then he looked over to see me holding my big duffel bag and Mr Grey's housewarming cactus.

"Oh," Dad sighed. "Give me your bag. I'm sure I can strap that to the roof too."

But I held on tight, not willing to let it out of my sight. I had managed to keep it through thirteen moves and an earthquake, and I wasn't going to risk losing it now.

"All right, you keep hold of that," Dad said, slamming the door shut with a wink.

As the van rumbled to a start, my heart leapt. We were finally going to our new home.

"So, our new home," I asked, "if it isn't really a house, then what exactly is it?"

"Well, it's a bit different to anywhere we've lived before," Mum said. Her voice was teasing.

All our past homes rushed through my head. The flats above noisy nightclubs and chip shops. The cold caravans on windy hills and by seaside towns. The houseboat on a canal where I'd watched little silver fishes dart below. I even remembered the horrible Easter holiday we'd spent in the back of Dad's van, before we moved to our trailer by a glassy clear lake. And finally, I thought of Verity Close and our neat terraced house, in our nice safe neighbourhood, where nothing bad had ever happened until we arrived. We had lived in every kind of home imaginable. I wasn't sure what was left.

"Is it a castle?" I asked hopefully.

"Or a mansion?" Billy said.

"I wish," Dad chuckled as we pulled out of the B & B.

"It's not a tent, is it?" I said, starting to get nervous.

"Or a shed?" Billy added anxiously.

"Stop trying to ruin the surprise," Mum said.

But in our family, surprises were never good. I felt my stomach flutter, like it was filled with all the butterflies we had seen with Neena. I took a deep breath and tried to steady myself. Billy nudged me and signed, "I got you, brother."

Billy seemed so much more grown up these days. He was still the mermaid-loving, ferret-trick-teaching boy I knew. But somehow, I knew he wouldn't have to sleep with his Batman night light any more. Not when he had been the bravest one of us all.

I watched the houses and roads I knew so well whizz by as we drove past. I looked behind me, checking one last time that we weren't being followed by the big black birds from the north. Just a little part of me still couldn't quite believe it was all over. But there was nothing but cars and trees and bright sunshine. Not a dark wing in sight.

Little Bamford was on a turn-off just outside the city. The road took us through farms and fields and over a fast-flowing river until we arrived at a village. We drove past the high street and the little museum and off on to a rocky uphill track behind a tumbledown church.

"We're almost here," Mum called out to us, her voice filled with excitement.

The van bumped and jumped until Dad pulled us to a stop on the edge of a mossy lane.

"It's just down this path," Dad said. "We'll have to walk the rest of the way."

Billy shot me a worried glance. And I felt my stomach lurch again. What were we going to find at the end of the lane? A hovel, a damp cave, a haunted house? I ducked underneath a thicket of trees and headed down a narrow dirt path until I saw it.

I stopped.

"What do you think?" Mum asked nervously.

I tried to take it all in: the low sloping roof, the big stone walls with neat cottage windows and a bright yellow door. And then I smiled. Mum and Dad had been right; our new home wasn't a house because it was a bungalow! But the most perfect bungalow I'd ever seen. The only thing that made me and Billy frown was the number hanging over the letter box. Number thirteen.

"It's OK," said Dad, squeezing my shoulder. "I

don't think we have to worry about bad omens any more."

And for the first time, I believed him.

Inside, the bungalow was small but perfect. And everything was filled with light. I felt the walls and ran my hand across the fireplace. Billy collapsed into the comfy-looking sofa.

"Has it got good bones, Mum?" he said.

Mum laughed. "I think it does," she said.

She went into the kitchen to inspect every cupboard, opening and closing doors with a loud *hmm*.

"It might need a little work," Dad said as a cupboard door fell off.

But I could hear in his voice how excited he was to have another project. A project that would finally become our home.

"So which bedroom is mine and Arnold's?" Billy asked.

"I'll show you," Dad said, leading him to the end of the hallway.

It wasn't long before I could hear whooping and the creaking of bedsprings.

"And this is your room, Noah," Mum said, opening the door across from the living room.

My room was just as bright as the rest of the

house. It smelt of fresh paint and lemons, and from the window I could see the garden. It seemed to go on for ever.

"It needs work. But we can make it nice, I promise," Mum said.

I looked around the room. Even though it was empty, I could imagine the wardrobe with my school uniform hanging in it. I could see the bookshelf filled with all my animal books. The desk covered in my Lego models. Neena and Liam hanging out here on the weekends, laughing and teasing each other.

"I love it," I said. I put the housewarming cactus that Mr Grey had given me on the desk by the window.

I couldn't wait to show Neena everything. But it would have to wait. After our trip to the butterfly house, Neena and her parents had gone on a trip to India. Neena had already sent me a postcard, a picture of a rare swallowtail butterfly.

I pinned the postcard up on my corkboard and glanced out of the window. Outside I could see Dad in the garden, trying to fix up my old bike, so that I could ride it to the bus stop in the morning. And I could see Billy spinning around in circles with a bright pink hula hoop he'd found in the shed. Birds circled lazily in the air. A fat wood pigeon cooed on a rooftop across the street. And, from the corner of my eye, I swore I saw the flash of a red-and-white tail disappear into the bushes. I smiled, and then I began to unpack my duffel bag for the very first time.

# ACKNOWLEDGEMENTS

When you pick up a finished book it's easy to forget that the stories in them often started off as wild and terrifying creatures. And that it takes many people to help tame an author's story into a complete and whole book. This is my opportunity to thank those people. Thank you to Lauren and Gen, word-wranglers and story-tamers. The Scholastic team, for putting the book together and getting it out into the world. My mum, the proofreader and no-nonsense opinion giver. Dad, the occasional soundboard for plothole fixes. Kelly for her ever-generous support and championing. Hellie, agent extraordinaire, Claire and Kate and the whole team at Janklow and Nesbit UK. The Portsmouth School Library service and the countless librarians, teachers and bloggers for their support.

# Have you read?

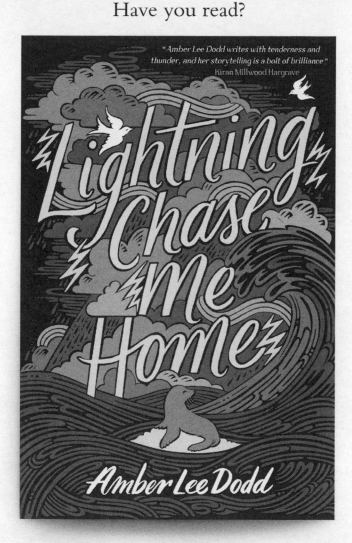

Turn over for an extract...

# Chapter 2

In bed that night I got out *The Little Book of Lady Adventurers*. I flipped open the cover and read the writing on the inside of the book for the millionth time.

*To Amelia Hester McLeod. Remember your name. Anything is possible.*

My mum had named me after her two favourite explorers, Amelia Earhart and Lady Hester Stanhope. Amelia Earhart was the first female aviator to fly solo across the Atlantic Ocean. She vanished while attempting to fly across the world. Lady Hester Stanhope was known as "Queen of the desert". She travelled across the Middle East on an Arab stallion, disguised as a man with a cutlass searching for treasure, before she went very mad. I think Mum thought naming me after them would mean I'd grow up to be a brave adventurer. But I'm not very brave and I've never come close to having an adventure. I've never even left the islands! And they are possibly the most boring place in the world. So boring that most maps leave them off. If you were to look for them you'd have to trace your finger up from the pointy tip of Scotland, past Shetland and the North Sea. And there, right at the top, just as the map is about to disappear, are my islands. There are three of them: Dark Muir, where I live, Sometimes Island, which is technically only an island at high tide, and Stony Isle, which is the biggest of the three. That's where my new school is.

I was trying to picture my new school. I'd only visited it once, and me and Da were running late to meet the head teacher so I didn't actually get to look round beforehand. Then I had to do a test and I felt so miserable afterwards that I just wanted to go straight home. I was pretty sure I had failed, because no matter how hard I tried, all the questions got jumbled up in my head. I've got this problem with words. They never seem to stay still. They're always jiggling about, or sliding off the page. It takes me for ever to read anything and even then I have to skip out all the words I don't recognize. Even Mum struggled to get me reading. I had to read over *The Little Book of Lady Adventurers* so many times with her, that I learned it off by heart. I still can't read it in my head though; I have to read it out loud when I'm on my own. So I pretend I'm reading it to Pipi, who is actually a great audience and barks at the exciting bits. Mum didn't seem to mind that I was slow at some things, not like Da and Grandpa. When they tried to teach me there was a lot of yelling.

*Amelia Hester McLeod, your handwriting is unreadable.*

*Amelia Hester McLeod, your reading assignment is woeful.*

*Amelia Hester McLeod, none of these maths problems are correct.*

*Amelia Hester McLeod, why have you stuck all the pages of your workbook together?*

I had got so sick of hearing my full name that I stopped paying attention and started listening to the funny ideas in my head. The ones that whisper halfway through a maths test to fill in all the answers with the same number, or to put sticky notes all over your face, or to paint everything with Tippex until you get dizzy. In the end Da couldn't stand it any more. And poor Grandpa had become more and more forgetful. Once, halfway through a maths lesson, he decided we needed to paint the living room. We painted the whole room bright yellow and brown until it looked like a bee's belly. Da was really cross with Grandpa for a whole week afterwards. So it was a bit of a relief to be starting school. I was finally going to be like all the other kids on the island. Maybe I would become massively popular and start getting invited to other people's birthday parties. Or I would discover new talents like being an expert gymnast/rope climber. And then one day soon Mum would walk back through the door, ready to teach me about all the amazing places she had been.

I buried myself under the covers with Mum's compass and wondered where in the world she could be on my birthday. Then I made a list in the new notebook Grandpa had given me.

Places where Mum could be on my birthday and reasons why she can't make it home.

- Brazil: Mum is lost in the Amazon rainforest. A search party of six strong men and five cunning dogs have been sent out to look for her.
- Tanzania: she's currently halfway up Mount Kilimanjaro. She intended to finish climbing it before my birthday, but her guide, Mwamba, broke his leg and she's had to carry him.

- Manitoba: she's having to hide up a tree from a pack of hungry black bears. A posse of Canadian Mounted Police have been sent to find her, but a blizzard is slowing them down.
- Siberia: she's in a sledge race with a Russian named Ivan. Whoever wins gets an ice palace named after them. She wrote a letter to me explaining she would be late but there are no post boxes in the wilderness of Siberia. Obviously.

Wherever she was, I knew one thing: she had missed another of my birthdays. I had turned eleven, I had touched Serpent's Tooth Rock and I was about to start school. But I still felt the same. I was still just the lonely girl who lived on an island in the middle of nowhere, who was rubbish at reading and didn't know where her mum was.

Little did I know all that was about to change.

When I went to bed that night, the sky was filled with strange green lights shining down on Serpent's Tooth Rock, making it glow. But I didn't see any of this. I had fallen fast asleep to the sounds of Grandpa pacing in his bedroom, the drip of the kitchen tap and the snoring of a terrier who had eaten too much of my ugly birthday cake.

© Kelly Boyland

Amber Lee Dodd teaches creative writing workshops, has a blue belt in kickboxing and briefly lived in a Scottish castle. You can find her writing in bed, the back of a bus, or in the corner of a noisy pub. Her plays have been performed at the Minerva Theatre, New Theatre Royal and the Edinburgh Fringe. Her short stories have been published around the world and broadcast on BBC Radio 4. Her first book, *We Are Giants*, was nominated for ten awards, winning the Calderdale Book of the Year and shortlisting for the Branford Boase Award. Her second book, *Lightning Chase Me Home*, was chosen as a Booktrust book of the month and featured in the Guardian's Best New Kids Books supplement.

You can find her on twitter and Instagram @amberleedodd and at www.amberleedodd.com